WHITE TAIL

WHITE TAIL
The Story of an African Buffalo

by

Ed Naylor

The Book Guild Limited
SUSSEX ENGLAND

This book is for Patsy

©Ed Naylor, 1983
Printed in Great Britain by
Charles Clarke (Haywards Heath) Ltd.
ISBN 0 86332 014 7

Contents

PART 1   THE CALF
1   The Man and Robert   1
2   Mukadi and the Fig Tree   4
3   The Birth of White Tail   7
4   The Island   9
5   Mukadi's Village   13
6   Death of a Lioness   15
7   Lessons by a Pool   19
8   The Trap   21
9   The First Encounter   26

PART 2   THE YEARLING
10   The Hills of the Rock Jumpers   29
11   The Buffalo Pool   33
12   The Fire   36
13   The Crocodile   39
14   The Killer   44
15   After the Funeral   48
16   The Diviner   52
17   Recovery   56

PART 3   THE ADULT
18   White Tail Grows Up   57
19   Chipimo   60
20   Death of a Warrior   63
21   Mudenda as Chameleon   68
22   The Fight   71

PART 4   THE LEADER
23   The Fishermen   75
24   The Rains   78
25   Hints of Danger   83
26   The D.C.   86
27   Waiting   93
28   The Chila   97

PART 5   OLD AGE
29   White Tail leaves the herd   101
30   The Last Big Walk   104
31   The Death of White Tail   108

Preface

Most of the incidents relating to animals in this novel happened. Some, the majority, such as the gathering of the five-thousand buffalo, the trapping and releasing of the waterbuck and the otters fishing were witnessed by my wife and myself. Others, such as the rescuing of the buffalo calf from the mud, were reported by some of my many friends in the Old Northern Rhodesian Game Department. A few, such as the death of White Tail, are fiction, but eminently feasible.

The country dominated by the big river is the same as ever today, but sadly the river itself has changed. The gap, so often mentioned in this book, is now the site of a barrage, and the Island, so loved by the man, is now submerged forever beneath the waters of the resulting lake. But the rest of the country is the same and, happily, the game thrives. The Ila are still there. The diligent reader can work out when all this happened, but for dramatic effect I have described the Ila as they were in the 1920's. They no longer wear their distinctive head-dress, though service in the last war in Burma has entitled many of them to wear the red feather, and some still do. Their traditional hunt, the Chila, is no more, and I was privileged to be at the last one when more old men died than buffalo.

I acknowledge with thanks the help given to me by W. F. H. Ansell, F.Z.S., Mrs. M. J. H. Beckett, B.A., Mrs. P. R. S. Green, B.A., J. S. Thompson, A.L.A., Librarian, Choma, the Librarian and Fellows of the Zoological Society of London, and the Archivist and staff of the National Archives of Zambia. I am indebted to two other people whose help was invaluable. Firstly W. F. Bruce-Miller, M.B.E., O.D.S., who was kind enough to read the manuscript and to correct my errors of fact as far as the natural history of Zambia is concerned. His encyclopaedic knowledge of a complex subject made things very easy for me. Secondly, my wife, who not only encouraged my efforts but typed the manuscript, as well as sharing many happy trips into the bush and to the Island.

Choma
Zambia, 1981

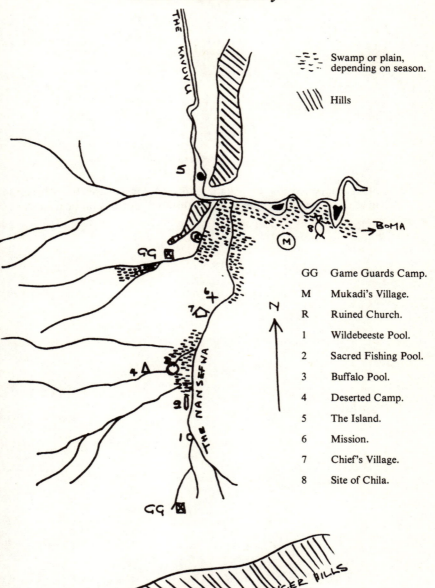

A Note

This happened not long ago, in the country of the Ila, where the Kavuvu, the river of the hippos, flows through the African heartland.

"This (buffalo) calf had a small white spot in the middle of its forehead ... and the terminal $3\frac{1}{2}$in. of its tail were white."

Game Guard S. M. Yamba
In a report to Puku, No. 3, the occasional
papers of the Zambian Wildlife Department.

PART 1   THE CALF

Chapter 1

The Man and Robert

It was difficult to see the man squatting amongst the rocks on top of the wooded hill overlooking the river where it poured through the gap to the plains. He was very still, and the dappling effect of the sunlight which shone between the leaves of the trees, even though it was raining gently, made him difficult to make out. The skin of his arms, face and legs was burned to a brown darker than the faded khaki of his shorts and shirt and battered bush hat. He turned his head slowly as he scanned the river and the bush beyond, his presence betrayed only by the glint of almost white hair under the brim of the hat.

Over his right shoulder was slung a rifle, reversed because of the rain. It was a double barrelled hand-made beauty from one of the better London gunsmiths, and fired a large bullet, heavy enough for anything that might attack the man. In his left hand he held a cromach, a strong straight piece of ash from his native Scotland. The handle, which was made of the antler of a red deer, had been beautifully fashioned by an old man who made a few pennies carving such things for the tourist shops. The man's leather belt and his calf-length boots were oiled and supple, and on the belt was a leather sheath holding the man's knife. It was no ordinary knife, having been issued to him when the man wore a red beret and carried a weapon more deadly than the rifle, dropping

White Tail

from the skies to help keep his Country's enemies in their place. It was now honed to a razor's sharpness and had many uses, being almost an extension of the man's right arm. The rifle, on the other hand, was seldom used now, though it was the best that money could buy. It was money well spent, for death can come swiftly and unexpectedly in the bush, and the man had used it often and well when he was younger and his blood hotter. Then he had hunted game relentlessly on foot the hard way. No Land Rover, no baits, no comfortable camps: just himself and his servant and the rifle, alone in the endless bush with the quarry.

He sat silently watching and listening, but there was no ulterior motive in his vigil. He wanted only to enjoy the sights, sounds and scents of the bush around him. A dassie, or rock rabbit, who lived with his own and several other families in these rocks, had dived into a deep crevice when the man appeared up the hill. He was the size of a large rabbit and distantly related to the elephants browsing far below near the river, and he now judged it safe enough to pop up his head to see if the coast was clear. His dark pointed nose twitched as his little eyes scanned the surrounding bush. He was in no hurry to come out, for he was wary of the leopards and larger mongooses which preyed on his like. Nor did he fail to look up into the skies for the shape of the eagle which could also bring death. The man saw him out of the corner of his eye, but was so still that the dassie neither saw nor heard him. More heads popped up and the dassie viewed the rain with mixed feelings. He knew that it would bring out the short, succulent, sweet shoots of new grass which he liked so much, and that it would lie in pools in the rocks, making the search for water easier, but it prevented him from pursuing his favourite hobby, which was lying and sunning himself on top of a warm rock. He whistled to his friends that all was well and began to nibble the grass, still unaware of the man.

A bushbuck barked sharply, once, twice, and a third time, and the dassies disappeared again into their bolt holes. The man knew that there was no bushbuck on the hill and recognised the signal from his servant and friend who was making coffee some 200 yards away, and who knew better than to whistle or shout. His imitation of the bushbuck's bark was excellent.

The man got up quietly, with no unnecessary movement. He adjusted the rifle sling over his right shoulder with one hand and took a fresh grip of the cromach with the other. He moved his binoculars until they rested under his left arm, the strap bandolier-wise across his chest, so that there could be no accidental clink of metal on rifle.

He was not tall, but his shoulders were very broad and his arms and legs heavily muscled. He turned away from the view and moved, still quietly, down towards the tree under which his servant waited with

The Man and Robert

the coffee. It was obvious that the cromach was carried for a purpose and was not there for show, for he limped on the swollen left knee which had received a few spent grenade fragments many years before in his army days.

His servant watched the man as he came carefully down the rocky slope, limping as usual but moving quickly and quietly over the broken ground. He remembered how the man had found him in the street outside his house in the small town where he lived, and had fed him. He remembered too the hunger and how he had been sent by his father from the wild village where he had been brought up to the town to earn money by doing odd jobs, and he remembered the weariness and the coldness of the nights. He had been 12 then, 14 years ago, and he had never left the man since. He was now the senior servant of five and a man of some importance amongst his fellows. He dressed well, even flashily in the town, but now he wore only a pair of shorts, and the rain washed gently down over him. He was no longer thin and ragged, but stood taller than his master, six feet of muscle, and very fit. He was doing the thing he liked best, which was to look after this man who was like a second father to him.

He had no trouble boiling water for the coffee in spite of the rain, having poured a little of the petrol he carried into the old tin half filled with sand, and lit that, as the man had taught him. The coffee was thick and black and syrupy with sugar and steamed in the two mugs.

"I see you, Robert," said the man, greeting him in the fashion of his tribe. "I see you, Bwana," Robert replied. "The coffee is ready. I have not filled the mug to the top as I thought that perhaps due to the rain you might like to fill it with some of the liquid fire from your flask."

The man laughed. "Thank you, Robert, but I see that you have not filled up your mug either. Put in some more coffee. There is enough."

"Yes, Bwana," he replied, but he held out the mug for the rum which the man was already pouring into his own mug, for this was an old game between them, one which they had played many times before. "Did you see any game?" "Only elephant, and I think that they will cross tonight by the full moon. And you?"

"Nothing, Bwana."

"Right. Let's move then. We will sleep on the Island. With luck we will see them cross."

The servant packed up the few essentials that they found necessary in the bush onto a carrying frame, which he hefted onto his back. He made sure that no trace of the fire remained, and, picking up his axe and 2 spears and the man's shotgun, moved off after the man, who was already walking down the track which would take them to the river and the Island.

Chapter 2

Mukadi and the Fig Tree

Many miles away to the East a wild fig tree stood at the edge of the grassy plain which led to the river. Huge and magnificent, standing apart from the trees of the forest 200 yards away, it was a tree of consequence. Only the tall palms rising in the haze across the flats had a similar dignity. It had taken 50 years to reach its present size, and it was a strong man indeed who could throw his spear clean over it now. The trunk was as wide as a tall man is tall, and the canopy was broad and gave good shade to many creatures. The rains having just started, it was heavy with fruit which hung in great reddish clusters. It was seldom without fruit at any time of the year, but in December it was always heavily laden, and its fecundity made the canopy a popular rendezvous, bustling with life.

Not being fruit eaters themselves, the 2 owls who lived in the tree did not appreciate the noise and commotion. The larger of the two, a spotted eagle owl with great ear tufts, was anxious about his mate, who was brooding 2 white eggs in their nest 200 yards away which they had built on top of an old nest abandoned by a hammerkop. He shook himself inside his feathers, fluffing them out, and decided that he must change his roost until the figs were eaten and peace returned to the tree. The scops owl was much smaller than his friend, but he had no intention of abandoning the tree, for having found and enlarged a small hole in a large branch he and his mate had built their nest within, and she too was brooding eggs.

The activity in the canopy which so annoyed the owls was caused by the fruit-eating birds who had come for the feast. They were all spectacular either because of their size or their plumage or both. Most active and perhaps the most beautiful were the green pigeons, who had arrived in a large party, an emerald cloud flashing across the sky and into the tree, where they attacked the fruit voraciously, even swinging upside down like the parrots who were already feeding there. The parrots, for all their ungainly appearance, could fly almost as fast as the pigeons, and were wise and cautious when they left the tree, always diving out of it almost to ground level before streaking noisily away. Tiny mouse birds and barbets were there too, and on top of the tree were the larger birds: the hornbills, who had come swooping and

Mukadi and the Fig Tree

swerving in their undulating flight; and the louries, the grey handsome noisy one sharing the feast with his beautiful, gaudy green crested cousin whose ancestors had fascinated a white missionary doctor who passed through these lands a century before, and who carried the missionary's name until scientists had given it a more suitable but less romantic one.

Under the tree, his back resting against one of the grey buttresses of the trunk, sat an African man, no longer young, enjoying the shade. He was an Ila, and as old as the tree, which was as old as the century now half gone. This was a good age for a man of his tribe, since death came easily and in many forms to these remote Ila villages; swiftly in the guise of a charging lion or the thrust of a spear, slowly in the guise of disease or famine or witchcraft. He had survived well.

He could not remember a time when the tree was not there and a part of his life, and he was happy in its shade, as though it gave him sanctuary as well as coolness. He did not know that the tree had been planted by his father, who, envious of the shade thrown by a wild fig in a neighbouring village, had broken off a branch and thrust it into the ground at the edge of his own. There it had prospered, escaping somehow the countless hooves of cattle which could so easily have crushed it, and avoiding too the depredations of the passing elephants. So it had lived, a memorial to the African's father, who had so enjoyed the shade of a similar tree when, as a young warrior of 20, he had emerged tired and wounded from the swamps into which he and the fighting men of his age group had driven the tribe's cattle to keep them safe from the fierce cattle-rustling Matabele warriors from the South. They, arrogant and proud, had followed the cattle into the morass and hence into the Ila trap. There their splendid Zulu tradition of warfare had availed them nothing. Helpless in the clinging mud and blinding reeds, they had been slaughtered by the young man's regiment to whom the swamps were familiar ground.

The man under the tree knew none of this. He only knew that he was happy there, and perhaps his belief in the force of his ancestral spirits had something to do with this, in spite of his ignorance of the association of the tree with his family.

There was no sign now of the village at the edge of which the tree had originally stood. When the primitive agricultural methods of the people had deprived the soil of all goodness they moved to new ground, and in fact had moved many times in the half century of the tree's life, so that it gradually became further and further away from the people's huts, and those who relished its shade and its fruits now had a long walk.

The man was not alone. His third wife, a girl of 15 years, was with him but apart from him, gathering figs which had fallen to the ground and putting them into a basket which the Ila's second wife had woven from the reeds. Occasionally she stretched up for a bunch of figs within reach and added them to her store. The figs were ripe and good to eat, even though most of them were riddled with insects, but this gathering was not for immediate use. It would be dried on the roof of a hut in the sun, and stored against the times when food was short, or perhaps as a treat for the children. By the time the fruit was ready for storing the insects would be either gone or sun-dried too.

The man was lazily but carefully honing the blade of a favourite hunting spear, which was called kapula, that is the silencer, for this was the spear he used to deliver the coup de grâce. It was thrown, but he also had a heavy-bladed short-hafted spear which he used for close quarter work against animals which he had wounded but which were still strong enough to put up a fight. This was already sharpened and was propped up against the trunk of the tree. Though as the finest hunter in the tribe he realised the importance of his weapons being just so, he was not really concentrating, and he had, for some time, been watching a large cloud of dust as it moved across the plain from the direction of the river towards the village. This being December and rain having fallen sufficiently to fill the wells, pans and waterholes in the vicinity of the village, the cattle were being driven back from the riverside pastures where they had been for the last 3 months during the dry season, and they were causing the dust.

Like all his tribe he loved cattle. They were an endless source of talk and speculation amongst the men folk, and he was anxious to be there when they arrived at the village to discuss, criticise and admire with his fellows at this big event of the year.

"Come, let us go back," he said to his wife, picking up his spears. She obediently picked up her things and the basket of figs, and balancing them on her head, strode after him, slim, and with magnificent poise, the result of carrying heavy loads on her head since she was a toddler, first in play, and then all too soon in earnest.

The village stood on a rise where the forest and floodplain met, and was larger than most, there being some 70 huts in it, though not as large as the great villages of the Chiefs, in which there might be 200. Circular themselves, and with grass and reed roofs which overhung the walls to give shade and shelter, the huts were set in a large circle, and with the stakes set close together in the ground between them formed a large protective fence. At night the cattle were driven inside, and most of the huts had adjacent small pens in which the owners' cattle were corralled. These opened inwards into the main kraal.

The Ila was the head man of this village, and he entered the main gate, which was in the west of the circle, and walked straight across to his hut, by tradition in the east and facing the gate, and larger than the other dwellings.

He greeted his other wives, and laid down his spears.

"After 3 days and nights I will hunt. Prepare for my journey and my needs," he said to his senior wife.

"It is not a good time of the year for hunting," she grumbled. "And besides, you are no longer young. Let the young men go if meat is needed."

"Do as I say, woman. The people are hungry for meat, and tired of pap and pumpkins and sour milk."

"Will you go to the flats with the dogs to hunt lechwe?"

"No. I want a large animal, an eland perhaps for the good fat, or perhaps if I am lucky even a buffalo. No, I shall go alone to the southwest towards the area of the fly that kills both us and our cattle and hunt along the river beside which are the ruins of the house of stone built by the white men for worshipping their God, who neither warned them of the fever there nor saved them when they became ill. I am going to see the cattle now," and taking a small skin bag of snuff with him, he walked over to join the throng at the gate where the first of the cattle were now arriving.

Chapter 3

The Birth of White Tail

The old female in charge of the herd of buffalo was feeling easier in her mind. Rain had been falling gently for several days, heralding the end of the dry season, which meant that she could lead the herd away from the open country near the river where the cover was scarce. They had been there, within reach of the water they needed daily, for nearly 3 months. Old and barren, she was wise in the ways of the bush, and devoted herself to the safety of the herd, which she was leading south to the forests where the water holes were now filling, and dry rivers beginning to flow. She left the herd bull, nominally the master of the 500 buffalo which made up his clan, to chivvy up the laggards, and guard the rear. The mass of animals did not hurry but grazed as they went, and in the middle of the day rested in a suitably safe place to chew the cud; but always they moved towards the mopane forest and the sweet new grass of the narrow, open places beside the watercourses.

The herd bull was a magnificent fighting and breeding machine, and

White Tail

he had fought for his dominance of the herd. Jet black, he was 12 years old, and huge, standing out from the other members of the herd because of his size, being over 5 feet at his shoulder and weighing $\frac{3}{4}$ of a ton. His massive head was crowned by even more massive horns, the palms of which met in the middle of his forehead to form the solid boss which, as much as the needle sharp tips, had ensured him the mastery of the herd. He followed his subjects, bringing up the rear with other bulls, all of them constantly alert with noses, ears and eyes for the lions which followed the herd as sure as night follows day, waiting for the sick, the weak, the aged and the young who might fall behind. These they would kill, generally efficiently and swiftly, but sometimes messily, cruelly and bloodily if the young of the pride were being given a lesson in killing by the old females. They had great respect for the huge bosses and sabre-like horns of fully grown buffalo, especially the bulls, and only out of absolute necessity and in desperation would they attack a bull in his prime.

Nearly a year ago the bull had served several cows as they came into season, which they did for one day every 3 weeks, and these cows were now ready to drop their calves.

By mid morning the herd had reached the edge of a patch of thick forest in which the old female had decided to lie up in the heat of the day, and she was now looking for a spot which would give her and the young sentry bulls clear vision down wind. Her acute sense of smell would protect her from every direction except one, and down wind she would have to rely on her vision and hearing. Eventually she was satisfied and the herd began to relax, apart from the watchers. Some stood sleepily chewing the cud in a half daze, whilst others lay down, and even the calves seemed to realise that the discipline of the march was relaxed, and they frolicked around, butting each other, skipping up in the air and chasing their tails and one another until they were tired and sought their mothers to drink and then sleep.

One cow was not relaxed. She was very near her time and wandered around a little way from the rest, grunting and occasionally rubbing her boss gently against a nearby tree. An hour before she had sensed that her labour was beginning, and now as the pains became stronger she began to grind her teeth and swish her tail violently, still on her feet, watched by the bulls who were her protection now she was at her most vulnerable. Quite suddenly she lay down, banged her head hard on the ground, and, bellowing loudly, pushed out a calf. The cord was severed and in less than 5 minutes the little bull was on his feet. In half an hour he would be ready to follow the herd and keep up with it.

He was very sturdy and even at that age he had a maleness about him, and butting fiercely he tried to avoid his mother's tongue as she

The Birth of White Tail

licked him, trying to get at her teats. Unlike his mother and the old bulls, he was not black, but a dirty grey-ish brown colour, which was usual in calves, but he was different from the rest of the herd in a way that was going to make him known and recognised throughout his life. His tail was pure white. By the time he had been cleaned the herd was beginning to move on, and unsteadily at first he followed, gaining confidence as he went, keeping close to his mother.

The lions who had been waiting down wind followed. The sentries had failed to detect them, and now they moved after the herd, realising that a calf had been born, and that both mother and child were vulnerable. They watched carefully for any lack of vigilance, but fearing the herd bull, kept well clear.

Chapter 4

The Island

The man continued down the hill until he reached an open space beside the river where a few waterbuck grazed. They glanced at him as he passed, but made no effort to move off, and when he came to the rocks at the edge of the river they already had their heads down again. He watched the water as it poured through a gap in the hills swirling and boiling as it went, suddenly becoming calm and placid as it debouched onto the flat alluvial flood plain beyond. The man turned and followed the bank northwards, until he came to the bank of a small tributary, and as there was hardly any water in it yet, he and the servant crossed easily. When they had scrambled up the bank on the far side, which was high and steep, for in a few weeks' time this dry sandy river would be a raging torrent 20 feet deep, they were able to see the palm trees which they knew were on the island 3 miles away. The route was now over flat grasslands. A mile wide, they ran alongside the river, only scattered patches of palms and dense thicket breaking the monotony of the grass, though the bank of the river carried a fringe of tall stately trees, under which it was pleasant for the man to walk. The level walking was easier for him, and the sight of their goal gave an incentive to move along quickly. On the far bank of the river there were reed huts used by the villagers for fishing, and these would soon be abandoned as the river rose to wash them away as it overflowed its banks. The surface was calm, there being no wind and the rain having stopped, and it was only broken by the circles made by the rising fish, bream or pike, which were

White Tail

very numerous. To his left a large watercourse, half swamp and half lagoon, meandered across the plain, the grass beside it fresh and green and closely grazed, unlike the unattractive rank yellow grass of the rest of the plain which had escaped last year's bush fires. It stood around in ugly clumps, and amongst it were flattened patches where various animals had lain up. Along the watercourse lived the puku. They too were unafraid and curious as the man walked past. They were not as large as the waterbuck the man had seen earlier. Their longish coats were a lovely russet colour, and the males had stout heavily ridged curled horns. The red colour jogged some part of the man's memory, and he had gone some way before he realised that it was the same as that of the red foxes of his boyhood in England.

There had been no sign of the elephants he had seen from the hill top. They had vanished, probably into the forest beyond the plain. Nor was there any other game to be seen, but the man moved now with great care, alert for lions and leopard. Nothing appeared, however, and presently they reached a point opposite the tail of the island where there was a large sandbank, on which lay a dozen hippos. The channel was narrow, perhaps thirty yards wide, and on the island rose the stately palms they had seen from afar. The man loved this peaceful and beautiful spot, and reluctantly abandoned the view to walk another couple of hundred yards upstream where there were fordable rapids, and here he and the servant crossed.

Immediately in front of them was the dominating feature of the small island, a group of 4 massive winter thorns, a kind of acacia, whose orange sickle-like pods, leafy branches, and, sadly, the bark, were favourite food of the elephants. So far the elephant had not ring-barked these giants, and they flourished. The large area of shade looked as though it would be a good place to camp, but the man knew better, for if the elephant came to feed this night no fire would deter them from getting at the trees. Accordingly he moved away, towards the tail of the island, and chose a flat spot with grass cropped short by the hippo, not too near the palms, whose fruit also attracted elephants, and stopped.

"Here will do, Robert," said the man. "Let's have some tea quickly and then we can get the camp organised." He sat on a huge fallen log, from a palm that had been felled by lightning some years before, and as he sipped his tea he took in the familiar scene, looking down the river to the hills where he had been standing a few hours before. He glanced up at the palms, thinking that they must be nearly forty feet tall, and was pleased to see a gathering of fast-flying birds in and around the canopy of fan-shaped leaves so far above him. They were probably hawking insects, and these were the palm swifts, who lived around these trees, even building their nests amongst the leaves, though generations of their

The Island

predecessors, having found the huge fan-like leaves difficult to nest upon, had evolved a nest which they glued to the sheltered underside of the fronds with their own saliva, and even when roosting at night they clung to the underside of the leaves. They were all active now as the afternoon drew on, and they wheeled and dived with abandon, emitting thin high-pitched screams. Their noise did not disturb a Dickinson's kestrel, tiny and fierce, who, like the swifts, was also attracted to the palms. She however preferred the dead stumps and she had her nest in the hollow at the top of one of these. She was sitting on 3 eggs, as she had done for 3 years past in the same place to the man's certain knowledge, sharing the brooding with her mate. Curiosity getting the better of her she lifted her head above the rim of the hollow stump, and the man saw her, and was glad, as though he had met again an old familiar friend, which indeed he had.

"This is no good, Robert. We must get on," he said. "Make the big fires here and here," marking the sandy ground with the cromach. "Make shelters too. It may rain. I will see about the food." He walked to the top of the island, and pushing his way through the sharp reeds which tore at his legs and arms, he came to a small bay some 20 yards across, which enclosed a deep pool. There was a hollow tree there giving good shade, and putting his hand carefully inside he drew out the rod and reel he kept there, safely for month after month, for this was a secret place and visited by few. On the bank opposite stood two palms and in the top of one of them were two fish eagles, conservative of habit, for it was seldom indeed that, the man came there and the birds were absent. The man attached a silver spinner to his line and cast across the river, a long cast more to get the kinks out of the line than anything else, but no sooner had the lure hit the water than it was taken, and by the manner and fierceness of the strike the man knew he had hooked a pike, and though this was very good from the angling point of view it was no good for filling empty bellies as it was so bony. The man beached it and killed it, leaving it at his feet, for it had another purpose to serve. He now began to fish in earnest and searching the river in a methodical and careful way, soon had half a dozen fat bream weighing a pound and a half or so each, on the bank. He cleaned them and then took up the pike. One fish eagle immediately became restless at the top of the palm, for he knew what was coming. The man threw the dead fish twenty yards or so in front of him, and sure enough down glided the bird, taking the fish from the river surface with barely a splash. This was another thing the man never tired of doing, and he was happy with the fishing and the bird and the day as he carried his catch back to the camp.

The servant had not been idle. Dead wood was scattered over the island, some of it broken from the trees by elephants, some of it torn

White Tail

down by the river when it flooded and covered most of the island, as it did every year, and some of it driftwood. There were many trees which had been pushed over complete by the elephant seeking some succulent out of reach branch and thus killed. He gathered some wood, for their safety as well as their comfort depended on it in the coming night, and made 2 huge rectangular piles about 4 paces apart, and, using dead dried palm fronds as kindling, lit them both. He then fashioned 2 lean-to shelters from reeds and straight sticks, binding them with the soft bark he had earlier stripped from a baobab tree for this purpose. He placed them between the fires. Should it rain in the night, as seemed likely, they would keep the sleeping men relatively dry, and the fires would make intruding animals think twice before coming near.

He did this work quickly and with the ease which comes with long practice, and was setting a battered metal teapot into which he had already put tea, sugar and powdered milk as well as water, on to the edge of the blaze to boil, when the man came through the trees carrying the bream. He selected some thick green reeds from the river bank and spitted the fish on them and stuck them into the ground close to the fire and leaning slightly towards it. He sat on a log turning them occasionally, enjoying the fire and the strong sweet tea, and eventually, after testing them with his knife, he was satisfied that they were cooked and handed 3 to the servant who disappeared into the shadows to eat them. The man scraped the blackened burnt skin from his share, revealing sweet white flesh which was a joy to eat. He wondered what Madame Prunier would have thought of this meal. He felt that she would have approved of the fish at least if not the manner of its eating. He drank his tea slowly and occasionally kicked a log to make the flames leap, sending showers of sparks whirling up into the black night. But it had been a long day, and feeling himself nodding, he crawled into the sleeping bag which the already sleeping Robert had laid out for him, and was soon asleep himself.

Chapter 5

Mukadi's Village

At the village the cattle had been back from the river pastures for several days and had been discussed and admired until the subject became tedious. Not boring, for the subject of cattle could never bore an Ila, but just tedious. The senior wife was aware of a restlessness in her husband, and, calling him by his nickname, for his birth name was taboo according to Ila custom, she said, "It is 4 days since you asked me to prepare for your hunt, Mukadi, and you have done nothing. If you delay much longer the flats will fill and your journey will become very difficult. Even now there has been enough rain for the game to be able to scatter away from the streams and waterholes."

She was a wise woman and had borne the man 10 children of whom 3 still lived, for in that wild and remote area only the hardiest survived. She knew the ways of the wild as well as Mukadi, whose name meant the Hunter. His skill and success as a hunter had earned him the praise name of Chilosha, the Spiller of Blood, because of the large quantity of game he had killed for his people. So he had 3 names, but the nickname was the one generally used.

"Enough, woman. You are right, but the business of the cattle is a serious thing and not to be hurried. I will leave tomorrow when the sun is well risen, and our son will accompany me. Now that his initiation ceremony is past he is a man and must learn to behave like one. Besides, it will be a long journey and I need his help."

The wife knew better than to argue, though her heart was heavy because this was the only son. There was in fact little to prepare for them, as they would be living largely off the land. She called her son and told him of the coming trip, and he, as is natural in a boy of 16, was delighted. "We shall honour your Father with a feast this night," she said. "Go and wet your spear, and kill a goat, for we need meat to add spice to the rest of the food. I have plenty beer brewed and there is also honey beer."

This he did and the goat was soon hacked to pieces and skewered and grilling over the open fire. Very soon the family and their guests had eaten and drunk themselves into a stupor, so that there were very few scraps left for the mangy emaciated village curs, though Mukadi's hunting dogs, who worked, and were useful to the community, were well fed.

The days when the Ila went abroad hunting stark naked wearing only their unique tall traditional headdress, which came to a point some 3 feet above their heads, and by which they could see where their companions were when the long grass was taller than a man, were past, and the next day the man was dressed simply in a loin cloth and a short kilt of animal skins, and in his hair, which was knotted on the top of his head, were 4 feathers, 2 blue and 2 red. The former had come from a lilac breasted roller and the latter from the bird they called the plantain eater, which was in fact the Livingstone's lourie. The boy was similarly dressed, but without the feathers, for the right to wear them had to be earned, and was awarded only by the Chief. The blue ones were awarded for some special act of valour, perhaps for saving cattle from marauding lions or people from an overturned canoe from a crocodile or hippo. The red ones were seldom seen now and the people who wore them were fewer and fewer, for the wearer had to have killed a lion, leopard, a buffalo, a mamba or a man. Mukadi had killed all of these, though he only admitted to the first four.

Even though they planned to travel lightly and took only the bare essentials they had plenty to carry. Each had a blanket rolled and slung across his back and shoulders, where the man also carried his bow and 6 arrows. The bow was as tall as himself, and he also carried an axe and 3 spears. From his waist hung a ball of twine and a roll of wire, both of which he had bought by barter from a passing trader, and which were used by him to make snares and traps. The boy carried more domestic items, a can which had once contained tinned peaches for water, a small skin pouch containing fish hooks, matches, and his father's pipe and tobacco, and a larger bag in which there was some meal, some salt, some dried figs, and some roasted mealie cobs.

Thus equipped and laden they set off with scant ceremony, the son walking slightly behind his father as was the polite custom of his tribe.

"Come and walk beside me, son," said Mukadi, "for today you will begin to learn about the bush in earnest. I will tell you which trees are useful and what they are useful for, and how to recognise animals by their spoor, and how to follow that spoor, and how to catch the fat barbel from the pools. I will teach you how to catch birds and small animals with snares. And what you learn you will remember, for in knowledge lies safety in the bush, and in ignorance lies disaster."

They walked along, Mukadi giving of his lore and wisdom, and the boy trying hard to remember so many new things, until they came to the last village before the tsetse fly and the game claimed the country, and there was no more habitation, for neither man nor his cattle could live

Mukadi's Village

there. Here they were hospitably received, and after much talking and good food, they prepared to sleep, for the next day they would be gone at dawn before the sun rose. They boy was excited and lay awake with his thoughts for some time, but Mukadi was asleep as soon as his head touched the ground, and, eventually, in spite of his excitement the boy followed suit.

Chapter 6

Death of a Lioness

The herd bull was uneasy. Though the lions had lost contact with the herd during the night after they had killed an old lone wildebeest bull, one lioness was still following the buffalo, and the herd bull's instinct was correct. The herd had been on the move since early morning and it was now nearly ten o'clock. The calves were beginning to tire, including White Tail, whose mother was anxiously chivvying him along. Some of the young bulls too sensed danger, and hung back to help their leader if necessary. The wind was blowing into the faces of the herd as they walked along, thus depriving them of their keenest sense as far as anything following them was concerned, forcing them uneasily to rely on their eyes and ears to detect the lioness which they suspected was following them.

She was, in fact, much closer than they knew, but moved carefully and silently, her greyish brown coat rendering her almost invisible in the grass and scrub. She was young and fit and hungry, and half regretted leaving the pride, but the calves were tempting, and hunger eventually overcame her discretion. She slipped round the back of the herd, still unseen, and worked her way along into a thick piece of scrub to the side of and just in front of the herd. A breath of wind blew across her back, and immediately the buffalo were alert, pawing the ground and snorting as they sought the danger they could now scent but still not see. She realised that she had gone too far and that if she was to eat she must move quickly, and charged at full speed for White Tail. It was fortunate for the calf that as she came he moved unknowingly to the safe side of his mother. The lioness thus deprived hardly faltered in her stride as she made for the cow, and springing onto her back, bowled her clean over. As she moved for the throat the last thing she felt was the tremendous impact of the boss and horns of the herd bull against her ribs. He tossed her high in the air, and even before she dropped awkwardly across a tree trunk lying nearby and her back broke, she was dead. The younger bulls joined the herd bull in savaging the body, tossing it and pounding it until it was pulp.

Meanwhile the cow suffered no more than some lacerations of her back and was none the worse for her experience, as she went forward to find White Tail who had made off into the safety of the herd.

This could have been one of those unknown dramas which happen all the time in the bush, but by chance it was seen and noted. The man had left the island. As he surmised, the elephants had crossed, using the island as a staging post. The first he knew of this was when, in the middle of the night, he was awakened by the crash of a bull elephant shaking one of the fan palms from which clattered masses of fruit, doing this in a methodical manner, stretching his trunk vertically and laying it against the palm, his tusks on each side of the bole, and then pushing backwards and forwards. This went on for some time and then the elephants moved to the vicinity of the winter thorn tree in the hope that some of the seed pods they relished had been overlooked at their last visit. But they were unlucky, and soon started to stretch upwards to tear down the fresh young shoots.

The man lay quietly between the fires, watching in the moonlight, and just before the sky began to lighten in the east, they moved off, and this was the signal for the 2 men to move as well, for the fish eagles were already screaming, and francolin calling, even though it was by no means properly light. As they drank their coffee with the good Jamaican rum in it they were startled to hear a loud screaming and barking on the bank, where a large pack of baboons rushed around wildly in panic. As they watched, the cause of the trouble, a leopard, leapt effortlessly ten feet onto the lower branch of a large msasa tree, dead baboon in mouth, and then made his way even higher. The dog baboons followed him into the tree, but kept their distance, and soon moved off, as though realising that their comrade was beyond their help. The leopard jammed the corpse into a large fork of the tree, and, satisfied that it was firmly fixed and would not fall, began to feed.

For a while the man and the servant watched and then reluctantly set off, crossing the river and then moving away from the bank, and after walking for half an hour they came to a well worn track, down which they turned to the south. It was one of those ancient roads, almost as old as Time, which criss-cross Africa. Perhaps it had started as a game trail and had then been used by long caravans of miserable slaves, neck yoked, driven along by hook-nosed men and their attendant black mercenaries. Whatever its origin, the man was glad to see it, for it made for easy walking. It was now light and the sun was pushing up above the horizon, and they were walking through deciduous woodland, interspersed with long swampy drainage channels, known locally as dambos. The trees were magnificent at this early stage in the rains, most numerous the stately Prince of Wales Feathers tree, so called from the fanciful resemblance of its leaflets to the Royal cipher, and the msasa, of the same family, and bearing small but beautiful white flowers. Amongst them were the occasional stately Rhodesian teak with large sprays of pinky-mauve flowers, so that the bush was colourful and fresh looking after the rain.

The game was on the move already and they could see many species. Unused to the presence of man it was very tame, or very wild, depending on one's point of view, in that it did not run away, but watched the men, curious and unafraid. Only the wildebeeste snorted and tossed their heads and cavorted around, but neither the men nor the other game took any notice of this behaviour, which was quite usual.

A honey badger hurried along the path in front of them, anxious to be home, for the sun was well up and he should have been safely in his lair long ago. He was full and happy because the previous evening a honey guide had fluttered in front of and above him, calling harshly, and had led him to a tree in which, high up, were the bees with their nest, the combs full of dark almost black honey. He had scaled the tree and ripped the combs to pieces, his thick coat making him impervious to the bees and their furious stinging, which would have killed any human trying to rob the hive. He ate wax, grubs and honey, and did not forget to leave an offering for the bird which had led him to the feast.

The honey badger trotted on in front of the man, his white mane and cape shining in the early morning sunlight. The man kept his distance and was glad it was going away from him and not towards him, for it feared neither man nor beast, and the man himself had seen one attack a kudu bull, more than 20 times its own weight, and he had heard that they had even attacked buffalo. Suddenly the honey badger left the path, and when the man reached the place where he had done so there was no sign of him, and he was probably safe in his burrow.

They walked along, and presently Robert gripped the man above the elbow, and stopped. "Vultures, Bwana," quietly. "Where?" "The-e-e-re," he said, drawing out the word and pointing with his chin, in the African fashion, to a large dead tree half a mile away which was festooned with vultures and marabou storks, standing out starkly in silhouette against the sky. The man looked through his binoculars, and said "There are more on the ground and they are so full they can hardly waddle. There must be a kill there. Let's go and look," and loading both barrels of the rifle and holding it ready he led the way.

The dead tree was soon seen to be beside a pool, where the grass was close cropped for forty or fifty yards back from the water's edge, after which it was long and rank. In the grass the man made out all that remained of a wildebeest — a pathetic pair of horns. They squatted beside a small bush and systematically searched with both naked eye and binoculars for the lions that they knew were not far away, but could see nothing apart from the birds and 3 jackals who were looking in vain for any scraps that might be left. Suddenly a lioness stood up in the long grass, walked a few paces and then flopped down heavily again, her movement enabling the man to pick out a further 8 young lions and lionesses, and, as he had so often done before, he marvelled that he had not seen them earlier, so obvious were they when one knew where to look. The lions gazed back steadily at the men for some minutes, but soon the combination of hot sun and full belly proved too much for them, and they lay down again and dozed.

The man made his way back to the track, and after walking for some time was surprised to see the spoor of a lioness join the path, coming from the direction of the kill. It was fresh, and he followed it carefully, and soon it left the path again, the reason for this becoming apparent a little further along, where the path was churned up beyond recognition for 30 to 40 yards by the spoor of a herd of buffalo, including calves, which had recently crossed it. The lioness had taken a short cut to come up with the rear of the herd.

"The wind is right, Robert, and they are not far away. Come on, and we may see her kill," and they moved fast but silently along the spoor until they heard the unmistakable noises of the buffalo herd. They saw that the lion spoor had lengthened as she began to hurry off to the side to come up on the flank of the buffalo which they could see clearly now. Even as they watched they heard the lioness roar and rush out, and then saw her high in the air as she was tossed. They saw the bulls savage the carcass and had a glimpse of the herd rushing off, and the man noticed that one of the calves had a white tail.

Being unsuspected in his hiding place and the wind being steady, the man settled down to watch, never moving a muscle, for the bulls were excited by the scent of the lion, or the exhilaration of the kill, or the scent of blood. He prayed that the wind would not change, for in their present mood the bulls would attack and kill anything that moved. His wait was longer than he expected. For 6 hours the bulls stood guard over the dead lioness, occasionally butting and tossing the remains, until, satisfied but still excitable, they moved off after the herd. A waterbuck doe and her calf were in their path. She avoided them and made off, but the calf was too slow and was savaged by one of the young bulls and tossed around by the rest, a thing the man had never heard of before or thought possible.

It was now getting on and the sun was on that descent which seems to be so fast in the African bush, and they walked to a good camp site nearby, where they lit big fires again, ate, and slept, falling asleep to the chattering and screaming of the hyaenas which were already removing the corpse of the lioness in the distance.

Chapter 7

Lessons by a Pool

Mukadi gently shook the boy awake, and they both shivered as they blew the fire into life, drank a little water and ate some cold maize porridge. It was still dark as they crouched there, not even the hour of the horns, which is the time when the half frozen herdboys can just discern the horns of their charges against the lightening sky. They finished the calabash of sour milk, a present from their host of the previous evening, and set off westwards, away from civilisation as they knew it. By the time the sun rose they were well into the wild uninhabited fly-stricken wilderness, and after 2 or 3 hours walking they came to a small river which flowed eventually into the Kavuvu, when there was any water in it to flow. It was not flowing now, and consisted of a series of pools, some of them quite large, and all of them covered with waterlilies, yellow and white and lilac, over which the lilytrotters with their grotesque long claws walked and ran, their white heads jerking and bobbing as they went. There were duck too of many kinds, and the huge black spurwing geese.

Mukadi knew the place well and had already decided that this was where his base was to be. It was very near the ruined church and houses of the early missionaries, and game was plentiful. He chose a site a little way back from the close-cropped bank of a large pool, and from it they could see the line of the short grass beside the water, etched in a brilliant green against the sere yellow of the rest of the plain, and beyond, in the distance, the edge of the forest, shimmering in the heat.

"Come, son. We have work to do if we want to sleep with full bellies tonight," said Mukadi, and taking his axe, wire and twine, he began slowly to walk along the muddy edge of the pool, his eyes glued to the ground. Presently he gave a grunt of satisfaction and called the boy up to him. "You know these tracks?" he asked. "Yes," replied the boy. "Guinea fowl, and there are many young ones, not long hatched." The Ila was pleased with the boy's knowledge, and asked him if he knew

White Tail

how to snare them, which he did, having frequently set snares whilst out in the bush with the cattle. "All right then, you set a snare here." The boy searched for one of the birds' main runs, and tying one end of the twine to a peg he drove it deep into the ground until it was covered, and was firmly enough fixed not to be pulled out by the guinea fowl they hoped to catch. The boy regarded his handiwork, and then laid the running noose flat on the ground, scattering some leaves and grass around it, so that the twine, which was almost the same colour as the sandy soil, was quite invisible. He threw a few mealie pips around the trap and looked at Mukadi, who nodded his approval.

"That is well done. Now we will go further into the forest and set some snares for something bigger, because when we start hunting the big game I do not want to be worried about finding food all the time. If we can catch a duiker or reedbuck we can dry the meat and our problems will be over as far as food is concerned." They made their way carefully into the forest looking for game trails, and soon found a suitable piece of thicket, criss-crossed with paths made by small buck. "This is a good place," said Mukadi. "Pay attention to what I do. Watch and learn," and he started looking for a sapling, strong but flexible, beside the trail, and having found one he bent it double to test its resilience and strength. Satisfied, he said "Cut me a strong piece of hard wood the length and thickness of your arm, and trim one end to a point, and at the other end cut a deep notch." He himself found another piece, smaller than the piece the boy was shaping, and after cutting a notch in it he tied a noose to one end and a length of wire to the other. The wire he tied to the top of the sapling which he bent down, and fitted the notch on his piece of wood into the notch on the piece the boy had already driven into the ground, so that the sapling was held taut and bent. The noose he adjusted so that it rested vertically and across the trail. The trap was terrifying in its simplicity. Any creature running into the noose would dislodge the notched peg and find itself hoisted either by neck or limb high into the air by the released sapling, quite helpless and fated to die miserably unless the hunter ensured a quicker kinder death. Mukadi carefully swept the area in which they had been working with a bunch of grass and sticks, erasing as many of their traces as he could, though he could do nothing about their scent. "We can return now" he said to the boy, and they walked quietly back to the camp site beside the pool, where they found that a guinea fowl was already fluttering helplessly in the boy's snare. They killed it quickly and went to their camp and blew the embers into flame and built up the fire. The boy was surprised to see Mukadi go to the trouble of gutting the bird, laying the entrails carefully aside, for birds were normally eaten guts and all. It was then thrown to the boy to pluck very roughly, and this done was sealed in a casing of thick glutinous mud from the edge of the pool and pushed well into the embers of the fire where more wood was piled on top of it.

"You are wondering about the guts, I can tell," said Mukadi, "and thinking perhaps that I am foolish to remove them."

That is so, Father," he replied, "but now I think I know the reason," and opening his small pouch he drew out a large fish hook and held it up, interrogatively.

"Right," laughed Mukadi, and fastened a good length of strong twine to the hook. "Now cover it well with guts and we will put out this nightline for barbel which are very fond of such delicacies."

This they did, the boy watching carefully as the father made doubly and trebly sure that the line was securely anchored, for a large barbel is very strong. Then they returned to the fire and talked, the boy becoming sleepier and sleepier as he tried to remember all his father was telling him, until finally Mukadi adjudged the bird to be cooked, and, removing the mud ball from the fire he tapped the now hard casing with his axe and pulled away the mud from the bird and the remaining feathers with it, so that a clean succulent bird was revealed. They ate the bird quickly and completely, built up the fire, and were soon asleep, wrapped in their all too thin blankets.

Chapter 8

The Trap

Mukadi woke quickly. One moment he was sound asleep and the next he was alert. The boy was asleep beside him, and he lay still, not sure what it was that had awakened him. It was still quite dark, and it may have been the cold, for it was bitter, and he was glad to see that the fire which he had built up the night before with the good slow-burning mopane logs was still glowing and throwing up the occasional spark. Whatever it was, he was now wide awake, listening and sniffing like an animal. He could still see nothing, but on the faint pre-dawn breath of air he smelt the sweet but pungent smell of cattle, and very soon he was able to hear the snuffling and rustling and the muffled lowing of the buffalo herd. There was an occasional splash as they waded along the far side of the pool, but they did not stop, and soon he heard them drinking on the next pool a couple of hundred yards away as they moved into it up to their dewlaps. The sky began to lighten slowly, for there were many dark heavy looking clouds, and the distant rumble of

White Tail

thunder, but the buffalo were already leaving the water and making for the bush where they would lie up during the day. Mukadi saw now that there was a mist over the line of the pools and he wakened the boy to show him the tail end of the herd as it made for the tree line. The boy tried to sit up to see better but was pushed flat again by his father, who reminded him that where there were buffalo there could well be lions. They watched the last of the herd as it disappeared into the forest, and, glancing at the pool where the herd had been drinking they made out the shape of an old wildebeest bull moving through the thinning mist towards the water. He moved slowly, head down, tail drooping, and the very picture of dejection. He was old and tired and had been only too glad to leave the herd which he had once dominated because the antics of the younger beasts and the skittering and playing of the yearlings annoyed and disturbed him. So he had been happy to go off on his own, and for a time had enjoyed the company of another of his kind, equally aged, and later joined a small herd of zebra before wandering off on his own again, glad of the solitude.

As he approached the water a group of lionesses rose from the grass a hundred yards from him and trotted towards him, grunting and coughing, not hurrying and not making any effort to conceal themselves. He snorted when he saw them and tossing his head, galloped away from them as fast as he was able. He ran headlong into the pride leader, an old and scarred lion who killed almost nonchalantly with a blow of a paw and a twist of the old wildebeest's neck. Pleased with the success of their ambush the pride began to eat, the old male first and then the others in order of seniority. Almost as soon as the lion began to feed, tearing at the soft flesh between the hind legs to get at the guts, the vultures and marabou storks spiralled down, some to rest on a nearby tree, others on the ground as near the feeding lion as they felt prudent. A few hyaenas appeared. Probably they alone of all the scavengers would benefit from the kill, since one wildebeest does not go far amongst a pride of lions. They would get the large bones and the skull which were too tough for the lions' jaws, but which were easy meat for them. The vultures might get some hastily snatched mouthfuls, whilst the feeding lions were distracted. They were remarkably quick at this thievery considering how ungainly they looked.

Mukadi and the boy watched the killing and the feasting and the scavenging enthralled. The boy had never seen lion kill before and Mukadi only a couple of times, and the spectacle fascinated him, with a mixture of awe and fear as he wondered at the display of skill and strength he had witnessed.

Presently in ones and twos the pride moved down to the water, and the scavengers moved in on the few remains. The lions drank deeply, the

The Trap

water reddening from the blood on their chests, until, satisfied, they moved back to the grass where they lay down to rest, their bellies bloated and pendulous. There they remained, half hidden.

The 2 watchers were in no hurry to move and were happy to wait and let the lions settle well before getting up and blowing the fire into life. They then cautiously walked the few yards down to the pool to inspect their nightline, disturbing the large white raft of dozens of pelican resting there. The boy's face fell when he saw that the line was out on the bank with the ugly head of a barbel impaled firmly on the hook. A few scattered pieces of bone were all that was left of the body, and in the soft mud was the clawless spoor of 2 otters who had had an easy meal that night. Mukadi consoled the boy, but was still reluctant to move far, being nervous of the lions and hyaenas, and they sat beside their fire for some time, eating cold cooked maize cobs until Mukadi decided that it was safe to go and inspect the trap in the thicket. Gathering his weapons he motioned to the boy to follow, and as he moved off, one eye on the distant lions, he tensed as he saw a lioness get up, but relaxed when she only took a few paces before flopping down again in the grass. He did not see the man and his servant watching the lioness, nor did the man see the Ila. Their visit to the snare proved fruitless, and after making sure that it was still in working order they began the long walk back to the pool. It was lucky that they came across a troop of vervet monkeys which took to the trees on their approach, for Mukadi was able to shoot one out of the tree in which it thought it was safe, with his bow and arrow. So they had food for the night, Ila being a tribe having no taboos about eating monkeys as many others do. Especially when they are hungry. Later, their bellies full, they pondered the interesting but rather fruitless day, and went to sleep hoping for better hunting on the morrow.

*   *   *

It had begun to rain steadily before daylight, and by the time the still unseen sun had managed to force some daylight through the heavy clouds it was raining hard. There was no wind, and the rain came straight down, persistent and inexorable. There was no sound of bird or beast on this dull grey, sodden morning, only the muffled drumming of millions of drops of rain on the grass and trees, and the occasional roll of thunder very far away.

In spite of the downpour both the man and Robert were dry inside their good waterproof sleeping bags, and they were remarkably well protected from the worst of the rain by the apparently flimsy shelters Robert had made the night before. The gun and rifle too were dry, inside the sleeping bag. The man's face showed dimly through the opening at the top, but Robert was still asleep and the drawstrings of his bag were drawn tight. Reluctantly the man got up and was immediately drenched, and after waking the servant he lit their petrol and sand stove and made tea huddled over it to keep the rain off. As they finished the rain stopped, and they packed quickly, shivering and anxious to be on the move to get warm.

"We must get out of here now Robert," said the man. "It is still 3 hours' walk to the Game Guards' camp. If we do not hurry the Land Rover will have difficulty getting to the main track," and he walked off a little way through the rapidly clearing weather to relieve himself. He stopped.

About a couple of miles away he saw a column of thick yellow smoke spiralling upwards in the still air. He called the servant, and even as Robert saw it, it disappeared. They were not to know that Mukadi had just dowsed his smouldering mopane log on which the boy had foolishly thrown wet grass in an effort to get a flame and get warm.

"Now we have a detour," said the man. "It can only be poachers at this time of year, and we had better collect them," and, caching their equipment except for the rifle and a spear, they moved carefully but quickly towards the spot where the smoke had been. It began to rain again, to the satisfaction of the man, for the sound it made masked what little noise they were making. When they reached Mukadi's camp the Ila had gone, but it was evident that they had intended to return because they had left their things lying under a sodden blanket. "Two of them, a man and a boy, and well equipped for a poaching trip," said the man. "They have not done well though, only a few guinea fowl feathers and a fish head. Let's follow them." And the man motioned Robert to lead, for though the man was as good a tracker as his servant, if not better, it did no harm to let Robert think that he was the expert. The rain had made tracking very easy, and they moved rapidly along the spoor, which seemed to lead to some dense thickets about half a mile away.

Mukadi and the boy had in fact left the camp only a quarter of an hour before, the boy walking a few paces behind his father as they went to inspect the big snare, very dejected from the telling-off he had rightly had about the foolishness with the smoke.

There were a lot of waterbuck in this area, probably due to the fact not only that the habitat was very suitable for them but also because their flesh was unpalatable to both man and beast, and as a general rule both 2 and 4 legged predators left them alone, though the beauty of a prime bull's sweeping horns sometimes led to his downfall at the hands of some trophy hunter.

A group of 20 or so was moving slowly through the rain, from the forest where they had spent the night grazing and dozing. The adults were all female and there were several calves 2 or 3 months old at foot.

The Trap

They were led by an old doe whose thick shaggy mantle was turning a greyish white with age, and she was taking them by a well worn track to the thickets which lay ahead of them to the pools of the river beyond, where grew the reeds of which they were so fond. She was going slowly for the beating rain, and lack of wind deprived her of her sense of smell for practical purposes and she was relying on her eyes and ears to keep the group safe. She led them up to and into the thickets, still slowly and her senses gave no sign of danger; nonetheless she was uneasy, for her instinct warned her that all was not well.

Her instinct was right. She neither saw the trap nor heard the 2 Ila hiding a further 20 yards along the path. One moment she was stepping gingerly forward and the next she was hoisted high in the air as she pushed her neck through the steel noose and sprung the trap. She bleated pitiously as she hung there, her struggles making the noose tighter and tighter. The rest were gone in a flash. Mukadi and the boy emerged from their hiding place, and as she became aware of them her struggles became wilder in her panic. Mukadi had a disappointed look on his face as he had hoped for something more tasty than an old waterbuck doe. He took his axe and stepped forward to give the coup de grâce, and as he raised it there was the heavy reverberating roar of the big rifle and the thud of the bullet as it buried itself into a nearby tree trunk, having passed a foot over Mukadi's head.

In Ila Robert shouted "Drop the spear and axe, old one, and stand still", and the hunter and his son were only too happy to comply.

The man limped forward, made his gun safe, and, after glancing at the waterbuck, which was still struggling and was hardly able to bleat now as the wire cut deeper, grabbed the axe and with a few blows severed the sapling, and the animal fell to the ground, the noose still tight.

"I see you, old one. I see you, boy," he said politely. "Greetings. you have been foolish, I see. Now we must undo the damage." Without being told Robert tied the man's left ankle to the boy's left ankle, so that there could be no question of a sudden dash for freedom.

They approached the waterbuck, now on the ground and still choking, but an attempt to sit on its head to get at the noose to release it sent Robert flying through the air, so, unpleasant as it was to watch, the man let the beast slowly asphyxiate and when it was semi-conscious all 4 of them sat on her and released the noose. They jumped clear, and she staggered to her feet, then made off drunkenly along the path, but after a surprisingly short time she kicked her heels and ran off in the direction the herd had taken. As they watched her go the man hoped that she would be none the worse for her mishap. The Ila were made to walk in front as they made their way back to their camp, the 2 of them shuffling and stumbling.

White Tail

"Well, old one, did you beat the boy for his foolishness with the fire?" asked the man. "You know we Ila do not beat our children, Lord," replied Mukadi. "We are not savages, but he will be punished when we get home." The man looked up at the sky from which the rain was still pouring down, and seeing nothing but cloud from horizon to horizon, he said, "You are lucky, old one, for I must get to my vehicle and have no time to take foolish old men and their even more foolish sons to jail. Where do you live?" The old man told him. "Go home now, for your hunting is finished for this season," and taking the axe he broke into small pieces the bow, arrows and all the spears except one. "This is for your protection, old one, on your walk back home," and turning on his heel motioned Robert to follow, and slipped off quickly through the rain to his cache, Robert carrying the metal parts of the poachers' weapons.

Chapter 9

The First Encounter

The dry black soil of the mopane forest soaked up the teeming rain until it could soak up no more, and became a mass of sticky thick mud. In this area it was alkaline and poorly drained and was accordingly very suitable for the mopane trees which grew to a larger size here than in other parts of the country. They reached upwards, grey and stately for some 70 feet, like the columns of the nave of some primitive cathedral, and in fact were called cathedral mopane by some. Little grew between and beneath them, and at this time of the year as the rains were beginning and the grass was still short, a man could see far between their trunks. They were now looking at their best, for the rain had washed off the accumulated dust of the dry season, and they looked fresh and clean, and the leaves which were shaped like butterflies gleamed in delicate shades of red and yellow and green. It was a lovely sight, but at this moment the clean looking floor of the forest was being churned up in the heavy rain by the buffalo herd the man had seen the day before. They had hurried to reach the cover of the forest because earlier in the morning they had heard a loud explosive crack in the distance, and though most of the herd took this to be yet another large branch breaking, the herd bull and the old female who led them knew that it was nothing of the sort, and chivvied the others on. They, old and wise, associated the sound with the sudden death which had come in the

The First Encounter

past to other buffalo, and feared the unknown. But now the herd was in the forest and they felt safe amongst the familiar trees whose leaves they relished in spite of, or perhaps because of, their oily taste. They were moving slowly now and the mother of White Tail was glad, for since her escape from the lioness she carried 4 deep bleeding furrows across her back and the bruised muscles beneath were beginning to stiffen. The rain was a very doubtful ally, on the one hand keeping the wounds clean and the lions far away, but on the other making a morass of the ground and making walking a real effort. She was near exhaustion, being at the very tail of the herd and walking in their churned up spoor, so that it required all her will power to pull her legs out of the mud and put one in front of the other. Behind and beside her, his white tail drooping and his thin unsteady legs having a terrible struggle with the mud, came her calf.

Presently the herd stopped, giving them temporary relief, and White Tail lost no time in butting into the teats of his mother, who began to browse on the mopane. They had stopped because the leaders had reached a road, or rather a cleared track which a Land Rover could use, and they were in no hurry to cross until they were quite sure that both it and the forest beyond were safe. The rain cleared somewhat, and the matriarch being satisfied she led the herd over in a rush, and since there were 500 of them they reduced the part of the track they crossed to a muddy hollow into which surface water began to run. White Tail's mother used almost the last of her strength to get over, and her son, refreshed by his drink, followed, and was immediately held by the mud and became absolutely stuck. He bleated and bawled as hard as he could, not yet frightened by this strange thing that had gripped him, but his exhausted mother either could not or would not hear, and staggered on, and the other females in the herd felt that it was none of their business. He bawled in vain.

* * *

The ceaseless rain was beginning to get the man down a bit. The going was heavy for him too, and he used his cromach all the time to give some relief to his knee, which was swollen and sore, but not yet stiff. The servant plodded on behind him, and though the man began to cheer up as they neared the Game Guards' camp he would be glad when this particular trek was over. Normally he enjoyed walking in spite of the knee, there being so much to see in the bush and in the air, but the rain had turned everything into a dull damp sameness, and everything living sheltered and kept as dry as it could except for the elephant and the rhino, both of which seemed oblivious to it. Even the larger antelope such as the kudu and sable and roan antelope miserably tried to shelter, backs to the rain. He recognised a particular mopane tree which he

White Tail

knew stood beside the track, and in a few minutes he turned thankfully on to it.

"Right, Robert, not far now," he said, turning round to speak, and found to his surprise that Robert had stopped and was listening intently.

"There are many buffalo crossing the road behind us, Bwana. I can hear them."

"I believe you," replied the man, mentally cursing the grenade and the man who had thrown it, even though it was the last thing he had done, for it had taken the fine edge off his hearing as well as damaging his knee. "All the same, we must get on and get the car going. We are already late," and was turning in the direction they had taken when White Tail began bawling.

"A calf, Bwana. Perhaps there are lion after the herd."

"I don't think so; if there were it would not go on bawling so long. I think it is lost, though the herd is not far off," and, catching the look on his friend's face, he said resignedly "All right, dammit. Let's go and look," and he turned again and went off down the road. They had only to walk a short distance before they came upon White Tail.

"Stuck and lost," said the man. "I wonder where the mother is. Look Robert, it is the calf with the white tail we saw yesterday. The lioness may have injured the mother more than it seemed at the time. This is going to be tricky. You are the strong one. Get it out and I will cover you in case the mother comes."

Robert did as he was told, which was not easy, for though the calf was placid enough it was heavy and slippery, and Robert found it hard to keep his balance in the mud. But he managed at last and set it down beside the man, who was looking hard for the angry mother he expected to appear, but she was not to be seen. They set it after the now disappearing herd and turned to leave, but the man found himself gently butted at the back of his knees, and as he turned to stroke the calf it eagerly sucked his fingers on the hand he put out. At the third attempt White Tail seemed to get the idea and looked after the herd, to see his weary mother at last coming for him. She eyed the 2 men, the black and the white, and the man had the rifle very ready, but after a cool stare she turned her attention to her ever hungry calf and made her way back to the safety of the herd, the calf following.

"That is a very lucky calf," said the man. "Only a few days old and had a near miss from a lioness yesterday and from suffocation or the hyaenas today. He will do well," and at last they completed the journey to the Game Guards' camp and the Land Rover, to face the long drive home.

PART 2   THE YEARLING

Chapter 10

The Hills of the Rock Jumpers

The Land Rover bumped over the uneven track as it climbed into the hills, occasionally giving a bigger jolt than usual when the track lead it over an exposed piece of rock, for though the forest which covered the lower country persisted it was thinner now and the soil had disappeared in places leaving the granite exposed sometimes only as small boulders, but often as huge slabs. The hills were steep, and the higher the vehicle went the more rugged became the terrain, the track twisting and turning like some huge red snake between and around the rocks.

The man had been driving for several hours and his back was sore with the jolting. His arms ached with the effort of holding the heavily laden vehicle on the tortuous, corrugated track and with the constant gear changing. Nevertheless he was enjoying himself because the drive into and through these hills was a rare treat in a country so generally and apparently interminably flat. It was 18 months since he had passed this way, and then in the other direction. It had been a terrible journey then, for he had been caught by the early rains. The few hours delay caused by catching the poacher and by freeing the white tailed buffalo calf had made all the difference, and the heavens had opened long before he reached the all-weather road. Had he not given a lift to 2 men who were travelling to the line of rail from the Game Guards' camp he doubted whether he and Robert could have got the vehicle through the quagmire which the track had become. They had been reluctant to help when the vehicle stuck for the first time, and only the threat of being left in the wilds to find their own way home had persuaded them that

White Tail

perhaps it would be better to lend a hand. They had certainly earned their lift, for the man had had to use all his ingenuity at times to free the car, only to have it stick a few miles further on. But now in August things were very different. The sun shone warmly, and this being the month of the winds the heat was pleasant and not the deadly enervating dessicating horror it would become in a couple of months time.

"A bit better than the last time, Robert," said the man to his servant jammed in the seat beside him. "Couldn't be better in fact. What do you think we shall see first today?"

"Warthog, sure, Bwana" replied Robert.

"Nonsense," said the man. "It will be sable, and we shall see him when we begin to go down the other side of this hill."

Robert grinned but said nothing, for this was another of their games, and always as they reached these hills which were the beginning of the big game country the man asked the same question.

Presently the track no longer rose, but began to fall away in front of them, tortuous as ever, and the man stopped in the shade of one of the infrequent trees. They had reached the highest part of the road, though there were still some rocks higher than they were on their right as they crossed the shoulder. One one of these outcrops stood 3 stocky small antelopes, outlined between the trees and the sky. They were about the size of labradors and seemed to be on tiptoes as they stood, all 4 hooves close together, balancing on the rocks. These were the Klipspringers, and their small cylindrical hooves, which had very small points of contact with the ground, were fashioned for these outcrops. Their coarse, wiry pelts were a delicate yellowish olive colour which blended well with the leaves and sparse grass around the rocks. They were very still as they watched, and neither twitching ear nor flicking tail betrayed them. The man was quite unaware of them until he got out of the Land Rover and began to stretch, when there was a snort and all 3 shot past him across the track in front of the car.

"We were both wrong Robert, whatever else I expected it was not the rock jumpers. We will have a break here."

Whilst the servant made the tea and struggled to lift the heavy bonnet to check the oil and water the man wandered forwards along the track a few yards, and gazed entranced at the view before and below him. The road fell away quite sharply and he had a bird's eye view of the forest canopy stretching away before him like a vast carpet, to the flats some 2 miles away, getting denser as it got lower. And a gorgeous carpet it was too, for the trees had their new leaves, and besides the many shades of green he could see the yellows, coppers, reds and oranges of the great brachystegias. The display of colours rivalled that of the autumn colours in the land of the man's birth, but these were no

The Hills of the Rock Jumpers

dying and decayed leaves but the harbingers of the coming rainy season. Contrasting with these spectacular but gentle colours was the occasional slash of vivid scarlet from a lucky bean tree in full flower, and much more rarely the loveliest of them all, the wild pink jacarandas.

At the foot of the hills the forest changed as the country became flat, stretching away to the Kavuvu which was 50 miles away as the cormorant flies, and the trees were now largely mopane and massive grotesque baobabs. There were wide sweeps of grasslands as well, but the man could not see this vista at all clearly, partly due to the heat haze which turned everthing into a shimmering greyness, and partly due to the smoke of the numerous bush fires, some of which had started spontaneously and some of which had no doubt been started by poachers. The man knew that the smoke would make for a magnificent sunset that night.

Some 10 miles away a massive hill, rocky, grey and speckled with sunlight rose in isolation from the plain, as though thrown up as an afterthought millions of years ago. This was where they were making for. At the foot of the hill was a lonely Game Guard's camp. This Game Guard got his water from a tiny spring at the foot of the hill, the beginning of a river which wandered across the flatlands to the Kavuvu, hesitant at first but gaining in strength and size as it went until it was quite a respectable size when it reached its end. At this time of year long stretches of it consisted of dried black mud or equally dry sand. There were, however, hidden in the dense thickets they gave life to, some large pools, deep and long, round which congregated the game in countless numbers, grazing bare an ever increasing area of grassland around them, so that it became a longer and longer journey for the game each day to their ever diminishing water supply. The man had come to walk along the river and enjoy the game, which was easily seen in August as the grass was already becoming short and no longer hid the animals.

A mug of tea appeared in his hand, almost without his realising it, so absorbed was he with the view and his thoughts, and he drank it and made his way back to the car. After asking about the oil and water he gave each of the tyres a casual kick, and being satisfied that all was well started off again secure in the knowledge that if they did have a breakdown it would not be for the lack of simple checks. Such a breakdown could be serious, and an unnecessary one was sheer stupidity. There was little breeze now, and by the time they had reached the flats and their destination, they were hot and tired and more than ready for the water offered to them by the Game Guard. He had heard their car for a long time grinding across the flats before he saw first its dust and then the car itself.

"I see you Bwana. I see you Robert," he said, shaking hands with them in the African fashion, first clasping palms, then thumbs and then palms again. "I hope that you will stay the night here before you go on."

This being a very isolated post and the Game Guard alone apart from his wife and children it would have been churlish to refuse, for visitors were rare, and in any case the man wanted to learn what he could of the news of the game in the area.

The guard's wife came shyly forward, bobbing her greetings and clapping her hands gently together with a great show of natural politeness. The children had no such inhibitions and the three of them, dirty, dusty and with noses that would have been all the better for a wipe, rushed forward and grasped the man's shorts, looking for the sweets they knew he had brought for them, much to the chagrin of their parents who were shocked by this forwardness, which was very much against tribal custom. But the man laughed and gave them a packet of sweets for which they gave hasty thanks before dashing off to the shade of their house to eat them, laughing and giggling.

"You spoil them, Bwana," said the Game Guard.

"Not really," replied the man. "I don't see them very often and I am glad they look well. You had better help Robert offload, as there are some vegetables and fruit for you," and a sack of vegetables was soon handed over together with a large hand of plantains and several large pawpaws which were nearly ripe.

"These will make a change from masukus," said the man, referring to the small yellow fruits which cover the small untidy looking trees which bear them and which are plentiful in the bush. The skin of these fruits was tough but beneath was a sweet astringent pulp much liked by both animals and men.

"They will indeed, Bwana. Thank you."

The man handed over a few other gifts, mainly food, but also some tobacco, and then they ate, or at least the men did, for it was not customary for the children and women to eat with them. They ate round a fire which was more for companionship than warmth, and arranged for the Game Guard to look after the Land Rover and other kit whilst they were away walking, until the man excused himself and went to bed, leaving the 2 Africans to gossip over the dying fire.

* * *

They were up long before the sun appeared, locking the things they did not need into a steel trunk which was bolted into the back of the Land Rover. The car was then driven up to the Game Guard's hut and immobilised.

Robert made up the 2 back packs, for this was to be a longish trip, and just as the fierce red rim of the sun began to appear between the mopane to their right, the man took up his load, rifle and cromach, and the 2 of them set off at a good pace, having 15 long and hot miles to go this day.

Walking was pleasant only for the first hour or so. Though the track was good the almost leafless mopane threw little shade even where it was not destroyed by elephant, but, resisting the temptation to stop, the man kept on until he recognised a large baobab which he knew was about 5 miles from their starting point, and there they stopped and rested in the shade of the gigantic bole, and out came the inevitable tea pot.

Chapter 11

The Buffalo Pool

The previous rains had been good and the herd had prospered. There had been many calves due to the good conditions, and there were now over 700 buffalo in it of all shapes and sizes including White Tail.

The grass had come through well and the rains had filled the empty rivers and pools generously. The black soil of the mopane forest held the water, making the herd independent of the Kavuvu and its larger tributaries, and the buffalo got fat as the weeks passed, grazing always westwards until the forest began to be replaced by sandy scrub where the rain was not held in the soil but passed through, leaving nothing on the surface. When it reached this country the herd turned and grazed slowly back towards the Kavuvu following the now drying streams and pools, emptying them completely, for 700 buffalo require a lot of water every day. All this happened in accordance with some inexorable little-understood time-table, and the herd would reach permanent water round which the grazing would have recovered as the last of the temporary supplies dried up or were drunk. The buffalo were not the only large animals following the water. There were large herds of wildebeeste, last year's calves well-grown and the females pregnant again, there were the zebra, not so numerous but voracious for water, and the elephant. Only the eland of the larger mammals was independent of water.

White Tail knew nothing of the instinct which led the herd bull and the other leaders to turn when they reached the scrub. He only knew that the sun was in his eyes on the morning march, which he did not like, as the herd moved towards the Kavuvu. He was a yearling now, muscular, active and strong from good grazing, with rudimentary horns.

White Tail

He showed the promise of great strength and size to come, and was enjoying his carefree life. There was plenty of grass, plenty of water and the heat was not bad. He played fighting games with others of his age and size, butting vigorously against his rivals, fearing none, until he would pick an opponent too old and too strong for him and be butted and winded for his pains. But generally he wandered along at the slow pace of the grazing herd, carefree and happy in the security the herd gave to him and the other youngsters. Even the lions did not worry him for they were content to follow slowly, not exerting themselves, picking off the stragglers and the weak and the old, having no need to feed off the main herd at all.

The herd was making for a very large pool which never dried. It was on a very small tributary, hardly more than a burn, of a river along which the man would walk, but very far from the baobab beside which he was resting. Some fault in the earth's surface had caused this large pool to form on such a small stream, and it may well have been fed by springs, for it was a mile across and circular, and its waters came up to a man's waist. It was a remote and secret spot, known to very few, and those who discovered it, at least the Europeans, were so fascinated by the wildness and the beauty that they told no one about it, keeping it for themselves to enjoy. It was deep in the forest and surrounded by trees, some mopane and some evergreens, and it was covered with reeds and waterlillies. But as well as the floral cover it had another one of birds. Here gathered every variety of duck and goose known in the country, together with the snake birds and cormorants, the pelicans and the cranes, the storks and flamingoes. A breeding herd of elephant 50 strong lived in this area of never-failing water, and their presence in the pool drinking and dozing disturbed the birds not at all. Some of the surrounding trees were dead, and on top of these bare relics sat the fish eagles, proud, aloof and beautiful, their white heads glinting in the sunlight, their yellow eyes alert for a careless bream or barbel, of which there were many in the pool. When an eagle spotted one he became the embodiment of silent power as he glided down, majestic and menacing, to snatch up the careless one with a backward strike of his talons as he passed over it, carrying the fish up into a leafy tree where there was more chance of feeding undisturbed. Occasionally the ducks and geese would suddenly leave the pond, with a rattle of urgent wings. Why they did this was difficult to tell; perhaps they became aware of some danger imperceptible to others; perhaps it was to visit feeding grounds, or what seems most likely it was sheer joie de vivre. Then the sky would be darkened and the glare of the sun alleviated by the thousands of birds, and the air would drum with their wing beats, until, at another imperceptible signal, they would begin to settle, first a fews and then in

The Buffalo Pool

great swathes with much fussy shaking and preening of feathers, until the pool was quiet again.

White Tail's herd was not the only one making for this paradise. It often happened that 2 herds would join forces temporarily, making a brave sight. These unions were friendly affairs and there was no fighting, but on this occasion 4 other herds were converging on the pool. The last of these to arrive came from the south and was travelling slowly, for several of its members were sick. Some had died on the journey and some had died as they reached the pool, their mouths and nostrils ulcerated and foul, and weakened by the constant scouring which which sapped them until they could go no further. But most of them were healthy, and the scent of the water made them rush over the last 100 yards to it to join the other herds, so that some 5,000 buffalo covered the pool from end to end. None of them gave a thought to their dead as they enjoyed the water, but they were not forgotten by the scavengers who closed on them as they dropped, the vultures and the marabou storks, the jackals and the hyaenas, even the lordly eagles, and of course the lions, who had not had to kill for themselves for days and were bloated with such bounty. The buffalo drank and were in no hurry to leave the water. Standing dewlap-deep they grazed the reeds covering the pool, dipping their heads right under the surface to get at a particularly luscious mouthful. White Tail had been frightened by the crush as more and more buffalo arrived, and had had a moment of panic when he became jammed between 2 large bulls almost out of his depth, but a movement of the herd freed him and he made for the edge of the pool where there were not so many animals and where the water was shallower, and there he remained, enjoying the coolness and the good grazing, and like the rest of the herds, in no hurry to move on.

Chapter 12

The Fire

Mukadi was getting tired of the reproaches of his senior wife, largely because he knew that she was right and they were deserved. He saw her approaching now, small and very stout but with great dignity. He knew she was going to start again on the subject of his carelessness and his rather too casual kind-heartedness, and he raised his eyes and felt sick at what he saw. The flats before the village which should have been a sea of waving yellow grass were black and dusty, the colour of an old sable bull's skin, for as far as he could see, with here and there a wisp of dirty grey smoke rising from some small tree or bush, which had been caught in the raging bush fire which had consumed the plain. Bush fires were part of their lives, but this one had been unnecessary and was going to cause great suffering to man and beast in the months to come.

It had been early in August when his fellow tribesmen had suggested a lechwe hunt to him, and asked him to organise and lead it. The women, they said, were clamouring for new kilts made from the soft skins of the lechwe does, and of course everyone was meat-hungry as always. Such a hunt needed organisation, for the younger men of several villages joined forces to drive the lechwe with dogs across the flats towards the swamps, running them down and spearing them, whilst the older men waited concealed near the pitfalls they had made near the water's edge into which the animals hopefully would be driven. Fires were sometimes lit further to panic the antelope. Mukadi and the other elders were against the hunt, pointing out repeatedly the danger of the fires getting out of control in this month of high winds. They wanted to wait until the next month, when the group of stars known to them as Bulhezi and to the white men as the Pleiades rose, heralding the beginning of their year, when the wind would be less; but the younger men, pressed by their wives or lovers or both, were vociferous in their arguments, and Mukadi eventually agreed, asking only that no fires be lit. So plans were made, hunting dogs got ready, pitfalls dug and spears honed, until one morning the young men and the dogs set off at a steady lope towards the countless thousands of lechwe, whilst the older men waited concealed near the water.

The herds were fresh at first and in the first rush of the men many were able to double back round the end of the line and escape. It was at this stage that promises were forgotten and some young hot heads began to light fires on the flanks to prevent this happening again. From the water's edge miles away Mukadi saw the smoke and watched helplessly as the flames, fanned by the winds, grew with alarming speed. It was not a steady wind, but was hard and constantly changing direction, so that before anything could be done the whole area was ablaze. The young men who had lit the fire were aghast and turned to flee, but the flames had already surrounded them, and there they died and there next day their remains were found. Their screams hastened the flight of the rest as they made either for the water or back to the village. Had it not been for the short heavy unseasonal rainstorm, of which the swirling wind had been the herald, no-one could have foretold where the fire would stop. Even the villages with their tinder-dry huts and grain stores could have gone.

No antelopes were speared as the Ila sought safety clear of the fire. they made straight for the water in the swamps, and of the many thousands only 3 fell into the pitfalls, now abandoned by the fleeing men, and there they suffered until the moon rose and the hyaenas came.

"Do not reproach me further, woman," said Mukadi. "My head was as empty as that of a squirrel, or I should never have agreed to the hunt. This foolishness has cost us our grazing for the year, and the cattle are going to have to be driven far to pasture now, which is a pity, as they have done so well over the last rains. The young men deserve the sore feet and legs they will suffer this year herding the cattle so far away."

"You are right, Mukadi," said the senior wife. "The cattle will suffer and there will be little milk, and it is important now that we plan well for the months ahead which could be hungry ones, though the millet is good and harvested."

"There must be no problems this year with the fishing," he replied, referring to the annual fishing ceremony which was held at the sacred pool of the tribe on the Nanzefwa stream, many miles from their village and which was a communal affair.

"What problems could there be?" she asked. "You and the others will go off as usual and that is all there is to it."

"No, it is not all there is to it. Last year we drank beer far too long at the ceremonies and then spent half the time we should have spent fishing nursing our heads, building our camp and hunting. This year the Chief agrees that myself and 4 other headmen go early to prepare a camp and hunt for meat and dry it. We are also to choose the site for the weir across the pool and begin to build it before the rest of the tribe arrive. When Bulhezi arises we must be ready."

Seeing the sense of this the woman waddled off to begin

White Tail

preparations for the journey. Time was short and they had far to go. Each of the headmen, who came from widely scattered villages, would travel with an attendant, and each couple would make their separate ways to the pool. Mukadi had the farthest to go, and being forbidden by the Chief to take his son, as being too young for such semi-religious work, he asked an old friend, Sikoti, to accompany him. He agreed.

They would pass the ruined church and houses near the spot where the white man had caught him, south through the mopane forest until they reached the grasslands just beyond which was the Nanzefwa. There with the others they would build their camp and plan the fishing.

A couple of days later the 2 men set off and the first day travelled fast with few stops and no diversions, doing no hunting, until they had covered half the distance to their destination. It was late when they finally slept beside their fire, but they were off early next day, making for an Ila village, slightly off their route but a pleasant place to spend the second night of their journey. On the way they saw 2 dead warthog and a dead eland. There was no sign of predators and they were unable to account for them, especially as the vultures were busy, and jackals skulked around the eland, darting in to snatch pieces of meat from the birds. They remarked on the dead animals to their hosts in the village that night, and the villagers themselves had seen similar things, but never any sign of predators, so that they had reached the conclusion that some powerful magic had bewitched the dead animals.

Mukadi and Sikoti had only relatively few miles to travel on this last day of their journey, and they wanted to hunt en route for food for the camp. They soon emerged from the forest on to the grassland, and here was much game, but half the day passed before they were able to kill. They came up with a warthog sow with 3 six-week piglets at foot, and, deciding to run her down, they gave chase and off she went tail erect and head up, followed by the young ones in the same half proud half ridiculous attitude. But she did not run well and it was obvious that she was sick, and even as Mukadi came up with her and raised his spear she rolled over and died, gasping and drowning in the mucous which flowed from her ulcerated mouth and nose. They left her but slaughtered the piglets which would not leave the mother, and a little further on Sikoti suprised a duiker in the long grass, so that they arrived at the fishing spot well supplied with meat, and were welcomed by the other headmen who had already arrived. They were glad to rest in the cool green dampness of the glade of luxuriant trees which surrounded the long dark pool.

Their fishing plan was simple. A weir would be built right across the pool somewhere near its middle. When the rest of the men arrived they would drive the fish from both ends towards the weir, which, being made of reeds, was half dam and half trap. The fish would then be speared or simply caught by hand and thrown up to the bank where others would kill them quickly, for most of them were catfish and long survivors, adept at wriggling their way back to the water. They would then be split and laid on frames to dry in the sun before finally being bundled into large baskets made of reeds for transport to the Chief, who would share out the hundreds of fish they usually caught.

But the problem at the moment was the correct siting of the weir. This was the headmen's responsibility, and they went without further delay with their helpers to do this, and after much debate chose a spot. Sikoti climbed down the bank to test the depth of the water, and it could be seen that it came up to his chest, and he shouted up to the others that he thought he was now in the deepest spot.

Chapter 13

The Crocodile

The man wasted no time at the baobab tree, and as soon as the tea was drunk they set off again, walking through indifferent looking dry forest in which there was little life, for at this stage the Nansefwa was young and its bed dry. Only occasionally did they see small groups of hartebeeste which took little note of them as they passed. He and Robert plodded on knowing that not far ahead was the first large pool of the river, and this was their first stopping place, where they would pass the heat of the day. The appearance of scattered waterbuck meant that water was not far away, and they began to see more game, mostly families of wildebeeste, and they passed too a dead eland, which was thin and had obviously died not long before of disease. Presently the country began to open up and the course of the river could be more clearly seen. There was practically no grass, as the animals following the drying river had grazed it flat for a considerable distance back from each bank.

Quite suddenly in front of them they saw 50 or so wildebeeste, or rather they saw their heads and shoulders, since they were standing in a depression and their sloping backs and thin-looking legs were hidden. This hollow contained the pool the man sought, and the herd had been disturbed as they drank. The pool was kidney shaped, 50 yards long and 15 wide, and held a couple of feet of muddy water. All the wildebeeste turned to face them as they approached, quite still, unafraid, and eyes rivetted on the strangers, until the men were quite close to them, when one of them tossed his head and snorted, setting off the others, and they all cavorted and pranced their way to some nearby trees where they stopped and resumed their watching. The man approached the pool carefully, but there was nothing else there, and then moved away from the shadeless edge of the pool to the cool of a tree set on an anthill 20 yards back. Robert joined him and they checked the grass and shrubs on the anthill for snakes and anything else that might inconvenience them, and then thankfully set down their loads and lay and rested in the heat. There was another anthill with better shade a little distance away, but they were happy with what they had and did not move there. From it 18 pairs of tawny but drowsy eyes watched them with little interest.

A few frogs croaked in the muddy water, but were silenced by the arrival of a pair of hammerkops and a saddle-billed stork. The man thought as he had so often thought before how aptly the old Afrikaaners had named the ugly brown birds, for their heads and necks were just like a hammer, and wondered at the beauty and elegance of the tall brightly coloured stork. The smaller birds were efficient frog-catchers and loved the fresh water mussels buried in the mud and began to search for food, whilst their magnificent cousin began patiently to quarter the pool, stirring the mud with his long toes and watching carefully for any titbit that might appear. A large flock of guinea fowl came down to drink at the far end of the pool, chirrupping and clicking importantly. None of the birds took any notice of the men, who seeing nothing of great interest and being tired, soon dozed off.

The man woke with a start, and finding the sun well into its descent, shook Robert awake and made to move on. He was checking his rifle when he glanced at the other anthill, where a large lioness could now be seen watching him, soon to be joined by 2 others and the 15 one year and two year old cubs. The man pointed them out with a minimum of movement and no noise to Robert and then strode resolutely away, rifle ready. The pride watched them go, and half a mile further on he relaxed somewhat. Robert's face was by now resuming its normal black colour from the dirty grey it had turned when they saw the lions.

"Close, Robert," said the man. "I wonder where the males are," and was amused to see the greyness re-appearing. But the man himself was annoyed at his carelessness, for they had been very lucky.

The ground was now becoming sandy and the trees fewer until they were replaced by grassland. The soft ground and his tiredness made the man limp and he leaned heavily on the cromach as he walked, and when they had walked for another hour the man stopped and looked carefully around.

The Crocodile

"There is the sacred fishing spot of the Ila, Robert," he said, pointing with his chin to a dense mass of heavily leaved trees a mile away. "The pool is amongst the trees. I can see some smoke too. The camp builders must be there as it is too early for the actual fishing."

Robert sniffed, for he was not an Ila, but a member of another an in his opinion better tribe, and he had no time for Ila superstitions, though he knew better than to offend against their customs, some of which were similar to those of his own tribe.

"Good, Bwana. I shall be glad to get there and I hope we are not going to have any more walks as long as today's in this heat. They are poor hunters though. Look at the smoke."

"I agree," the man replied, "but to be fair they are not hunting, only camp building," and Robert sniffed again, and the man led off on the last stage of the day's journey.

* * *

The crocodile was old and big. Since the end of the last rains when he had failed to follow down the rapidly falling river to the big pools at its lower end he had been living in the sacred fishing pool. He had explored several other pools in the area, walking over land at surprising speed from pool to pool, but was disinclined to make the longer journey to his usual dry season home, and had returned to the fishing pool eventually because it was the biggest and deepest of the local ones. He had lived on the catfish in the pool, and once he had killed a waterbuck ram which had come down to drink at one of the few places where there was access to the water, knocking him into the water with one sweep of his tail. Its remains were tucked amongst the roots of a large trichilia tree which had been exposed to erosion, and soon the tree itself would be undermined and die too. The crocodile was not hungry, but missed, in this land of no rocks, finding a good stone or two to swallow to help his digestion.

This particular day he had been disturbed. Men had arrived on the bank and their chatter and the noise of their axes annoyed him. Several times they had come to the edge, arguing, pointing and gesticulating, but they had not seen him as he lay under the overhanging far bank, near the roots of the trichilia, quite still, only eyes and nostrils showing above the water. They went away, but not far for he could still hear them, and in the evening they returned, more of them now, and noisier than ever until finally one of them climbed down the bank into the pool, looking up and talking to his companions on the bank whose eyes were fixed on him.

The crocodile submerged further, and the whole fifteen feet of him slid without a ripple under the water until it seized Sikoti, pulling him under so fast that he had no time to scream. He was dragged across to the roots into which he was tucked next to the remains of the waterbuck, and where he would have drowned had he not first bled to death from a torn artery. A few spears fell harmlessly near the crocodile, but the horrified watchers on the bank, though they realised what had happened, never saw Sikoti again.

* * *

The man and Robert were walking slowly now and were very tired as they approached the fishing camp, but they were still alert and moving quietly when they became aware that there was some sort of commotion at the camp. Men were shouting and wailing and seemed to be rushing about aimlessly, so they hurried on and the Ila hardly noticed them arrive until the man said "I see you Mukadi, I see your friends. What is wrong?"

"Ah, I see you Bwana, I see you Robert," was the reply, and he seemed relieved as well as pleased to see them.

"What heavy thing has happened that you are wailing and in distress?" said the man. "Is someone dead?"

Mukadi told him the grim story, and the man felt the revulsion all hunters feel when one of them is taken by a crocodile. Let someone be taken by a lion or savaged by an elephant and it is felt to be sad but understandable and a price that every hunter knows he may have to pay one day. At least the victim looked death in the face. But being snatched by stealth and drowned is, illogically enough, not the same.

"We grieve for you, Mukadi, but we cannot help Sikoti now, but with any luck I can avenge him," and the man went to his own camp a little way off.

Tea was ready. "Tell Mukadi I want him, Robert. And get an extra cup for him."

When he arrived he was seated and given hot sweet tea, and the man said, "how are your cattle, and your wives and your boy? We saw your smoke from a long way off today".

Mukadi smiled as he noticed that the man had got his priorities right in his questioning.

"The cattle are all right at present and my wives are fat and talk too much. The boy is wilful but learns and remembers. And you know," he added reproachfully, "that we are not poaching and there is no need to hide our smoke. But I am worried, for the Spirits are worrying me and I am suffering," and he told the man of the fire and the loss of his grazing and again of the loss of his friend.

The man was sympathetic, adding "My people have a saying that misfortunes come in threes. Let us hope that it does not apply to you."

The Crocodile

"I hope not, Bwana, but the presence of the crocodile in the pool is not good, apart from Sikoti, for he must have been there since the rains ended, and he must have taken most of the fish, and that matters this year. But I must return alone and fast tomorrow to tell the Chief and then Sikoti's wife the bad news. Another thing, Bwana. The game is not all right, and I have seen many dead animals which have been killed by spirits, for neither lion nor leopard has touched them."

The man remembered the dead eland and they chatted for a little while, and then the man said, "Tell your people I will kill the crocodile when the moon is there," and he pointed to a quadrant of the sky with outstretched arm, squinting along it in the native fashion. "There must be no noise and no light from any fire."

Later on that evening when all was dark and silent under the young moon, the man and Robert lay on the bank, and when all was ready the man switched on a powerful torch searching methodically along the edge of the pool for the two red spots which would be the crocodile's eyes, and sure enough they were soon seen, on the opposite water's edge not 15 yards away. Robert slowly and carefully took the torch and held the reflections in its beam whilst the man readied the heavy rifle, and, using the faint moonlight which the ivory foresight reflected, the man took careful aim and fired. The shot was good and the big bullet blew off the reptile's head, but they did not find the body until the next day.

There was much rejoicing after the shot, with much talk and gorging with meat round the now big fires, and the story of the killing of the crocodile and the noise of the huge rifle was told and enacted repeatedly. Only Mukadi sat aside from the others thinking of his dead friend.

Chapter 14

The Killer

The buffalo were still at the big pool and were still in no hurry to leave the neighbourhood with its lush grazing and plentiful water. Most of the birds had gone, for 5,000 buffalo cover a large area, and there was neither room nor comfort for them amongst the constantly moving legs of the herd. So the water birds had left, winging their way out in great flights to other less crowded pools or even as far as the sand banks and islands of the Kavuvu itself. The fish eagles were still there even though they had to fish in the middle of the day when some of the buffalo went off to the forests for shade, and of course the swarms of snowy cattle egrets remained. These birds, of dazzling whiteness, familiar wherever buffalo are to be found, live on the insects which the great beasts disturb as they move and on the many ticks which, full of glutinous blood, fall from them, their yellow beaks flashing in the grass as they feed. Even the ticks not yet bloated are not safe, for the birds flutter up on to the buffaloes' backs seeking them out from the crevices in the skin, and relieving the buffalo of some of the irritation the ticks caused. The egrets were very beautiful as they strutted around the herd like constantly moving and shimmering carpets. Occasionally some small animal scuttering through the grass would disturb them, and then they would flutter a few feet up into the air before resuming their endless search for food. Only when the light began to fade did they take off, flying in huge silent flocks, in formation like the great geese of the Arctic, to their secret roosts, which were often in dead trees in the middle of a pool or beside a river. It was difficult to believe that trees, especially dead ones, could support such a weight of birds without breaking, but they did, and a distant watcher saw what appeared to be a white tree, which slowly turned to a dull pink as the sun finally set, and the squawking, squabbling and shuffling finally stilled until the next morning, when, first in ones and twos and then in large clouds, the birds would leave to find the herd again.

Amidst all the activity at the pool life was wonderful for White Tail, with all the new sights to see and plenty of friends to play with. His mother was still there, and though he had begun to forget her he was still never far from her if some new strangeness frightened him, or his dignity or feelings were hurt when the games got too rough. But he soon forgot his fright and his hurts and was off again, playing and exploring. He was tolerated by the cows as he did not yet worry them when they were in season, and his sexual immaturity saved him from the attentions of the bulls, which would come all too soon. So he ate and frolicked and slept. Sometimes he had differences of opinion with animals of other species which also used the pool, like the time when he went to drink at the edge of the water at a bare spot much favoured by an old bull elephant who lived alone in the vicinity of the breeding herd for company, his breeding days over. White Tail was startled to find this huge animal confronting him as it came down to the water as he turned to leave. He faced it for a second or two, but a couple of shakes of the massive head accompanied by a loud blowing through the searching trunk was enough to send the small buffalo crashing back to the rest of the herd. Not so the blacksmith's plover, so called because of its tinking cry which resembles the sound of hammer striking anvil. He also wanted to drink and made such a noise and gave such a demonstration that the surprised bull stopped, and after considering his tiny adversary for a few moments decided that a quiet life is best and turned away to seek another spot, whilst the small black and white bird continued to pretend he was a fierce eagle.

* * *

The walk through the grasslands was pleasant, and the serenity of the scene and the placidity of the game did something to erase the horror of Sikoti's death. As usual the man had left before light, and he and his servant were amongst the fecund herds of the grasslands before it was light and before the heavy mist had lifted, a mist that was there almost until the very end of the dry season, for in the wet these were swamps. Everywhere there was game: wildebeeste, reed buck and zebra, and in the distance elephant, and the man marvelled that they were in roughly the same areas as they had been in for many years, so that he was able to say to Robert "Just past that big anthill in front, the one with the red kaffir boom on it, there will be so and so," or "Beyond the next line of trees there will be something else," and there, nine times out of ten they would be. Robert had ceased to wonder at this, having decided years ago that his Bwana was a very powerful wizard.

They were early enough to have the chance of seeing nocturnal animals who might be delayed in getting home, but they were unlucky. All they saw was a serval cat carrying a dead guinea fowl, its feathers still wet from the dew. The man was glad however to see roan antelope around in large numbers, keeping closer to the river than most animals. Many thought that this large handsome antelope was declining seriously in numbers, but others, like the man, felt that there were just as many roan, but that they had been pushed farther back into the bush by the slowly spreading tentacles of civilisation. The man passed four groups of them, each of about twenty animals and all with calves. They lived undisturbed by lions most of the time, being fierce fighters, using their scimitar-like horns to good effect when necessary, slashing too at their molestors with sharp front hooves, the way the red deer do in the rut in Scotland. They were much fiercer than their cousins the sable who, though they had got longer, often enormous horns, lacked the pugnacity of the roan. The lions avoided both, wisely. However, there was nothing pugnacious about them this morning as they watched the man walk past less than fifty yards away, flicking their donkey-like ears, black and white faces alert. The impala with them were not so placid and skittered about nervously until the men were gone.

The only thing spoiling this idyllic walk was the number of dead animals mostly buffalo, that were seen. Vultures were everywhere, most of them too heavy to fly and resting in the trees and on the ground, Hyaenas with pendulous bellies sloped around in broad daylight, and there were many normally shy jackal to be seen. The lions too had got the message of the bounty there for the taking, and many were seen bloated and lazy. Even the cubs were full, which was a change for usually they got only the scraps left by the adults if they were lucky, and died frequently from hunger. Every quarter mile or so they saw a dead animal, and the man now realised that it was an epidemic of some kind that was killing them, and decided to push on to the radio at the Game Guards' camp to the north, and contact the Game Department vets and biologists, for if the disease was what he suspected they were going to have their hands full.

The man began to walk away from the Nanzefwa, leaving the track he used his map and compass, and being satisfied with his bearing he struck off towards the forest, an hour's walk away. Eventually they reached the area of the buffalo pool. "Quiet now Robert. There are often buffalo at this pool, and from the number of dead ones we have seen a herd was coming this way," and going forward through a thicket and round an anthill he said softly "Just in front now, Robert," and then Robert heard him give a gasp of wonder, and stepping up to his master drank in the view of the sea of buffalo covering the pool.

For several moments the man was speechless, and then said "I don't think anyone this century has ever seen so many buffalo together at one time, Robert. Look well for we may never see anything like this ever again," and getting themselves well hidden and comfortable the man sat down to watch. There were buffalo as far as the eye could see, and over on the other side was a bull elephant coming down to drink, demonstrating as he came and eventually turning away, but the man

The Killer

could not see why, even through his good glasses. The man sat fascinated, and then his heart sank, for this congregation was ideal for the rapid spread of whatever disease was killing the game, and he knew that there was nothing to be done.

They watched until the egrets began to move, and then turned westwards for the two mile walk to a deserted and abandoned Game Guards' camp which was in perfectly good order. Two Game Guards used to live there with a cook and a couple of carriers, and what happened no-one will ever know, but the Game Guards died and the carriers fled, accusing the cook of murder by witchcraft. This he indignantly denied to the Court which eventually tried him, and which acquitted him for lack of evidence. To prove his point he went back to the camp, now reputed to be both bewitched and haunted, and went back to sleep in his old house. It was a long sleep, for in the night for no reason that any white man could explain and old elephant bull tore down the hut the cook was in, unusual in itself, and killed him. No one would now go near the place, at least no Ila, and Robert was not very happy about it even though he was from another tribe. But his master's will prevailed and they slept comfortably in the other huts which were sound and dry, sharing them with the bats and ants and termites which were taking over. Even Robert slept well.

* * *

Next morning the man passed the pool on his way to the Game Guards' post to the north. The herd was still there, but there were now many more obviously sick animals in it, and the surrounds of the pool were littered with dead and dying, all with the terrible ulcerations of their mouths and nostrils, and lying passing their last hours in a sea of their own bloody faeces. The stench was appalling, and such animals as were not already affected were moving out of the area in a tired, listless way, for many of them were incubating the disease. The man was in a hurry now to get to the radio, and he passed the survivors, moving round the edge of the weary buffalo who were too exhausted to worry. It was then that they saw White Tail. He looked fitter than most and could occasionally trot, but spent his time in the vicinity of an old obviously very sick cow. As they watched she lay down, and White Tail saw the men, came aggresively towards them only to stop twenty yards away, look and give a snort and return to the now almost dead cow, and, apparently realising the inevitable, he gave a low bellow, almost a moan, and went wearily after the herd, his dead mother soon forgotten.

"That animal was born lucky," said the man to Robert, for he had recognised White Tail. "Remember when the lioness missed him, and when we pulled him out of the mud? I shouldn't be surprised if he survives this too. I wonder if he recognised us as his rescuers and that is why he stopped. It is a nice thought."

White Tail did survive, one of only about 400 out of the 5,000, and these divided up into four groups, White Tail joining one which went up to the grasslands opposite the island to recuperate and recover.

Chapter 15

After the Funeral

By dint of some very hard walking they arrived at the Game Guards' camp to the north of them that evening, but were too late for the radio schedule and had to wait until the morning. They were glad of the long sleep. The Wild Life Department came on the air on schedule, but radios in those days were not very sophisticated and a great deal of patience was needed both to hear and to make oneself heard through the constant crackling and fading, but eventually the biologist the man wanted came on the set. He was also a vet. The man put him in the picture and then said, "It looks like rinderpest to me, Dick. I can't think what else it can be. But that's impossible isn't it?"

"Well, there has not been an outbreak of any size for over 50 years," his friend replied, and even over the air the man could sense the worry in his voice, "but ther are rumours of it in East Africa."

"Why not drive down here?" said the man. "You can cross the Kavuvu by the pontoon and drive across the flats and I will meet you at Mukadi's village; the Ila cattle must be affected too. You can see for yourself then, and you could drive me through the country I have just walked through, back to my car, and you can see what the game is like. And after that, if I am right, the best of luck to you. I wouldn't like to be in your shoes. I'm glad it's not my worry." The man meant it too, for rinderpest is deadly and highly contagious, and if it started amongst domestic cattle with the violence it had shown among the wild, Dick and every other vet in the country was going to have his hands full.

A few final words confirmed map references, distances and times. They estimated that it would take the man two days to walk to Mukadi's, the same as it would take the vet to get organised and drive there from the capital, and so they agreed to meet at the village on the morning of the third day.

There was no reason to wait, and after breakfast they set off for the rather leisurely two days' walk, which was uneventful, apart from the

After the Funeral

now familiar dead animals. The man enjoyed the walk in spite of this depressing feature. He had taken a liking to Mukadi. He was pleased that the old Ila had borne him no ill will for capturing him and destroying his weapons, and beneath his dust and dirt and poor clothing the man realised that there was a leader, and possibly a steadfast friend. The second day's walking was the same except that they now began to see dead cattle as well as dead game as they neared the villages.

The man thought of shooting a hartebeeste as a gift for the villagers, but quickly abandoned the idea when he remembered that they had no qualms about eating the cattle dying around them. Not to eat them would be considered at the best eccentric and at the worst a sign of guilt, and anyone not eating could quite well be suspected of bewitching the cattle and causing them to die in the first place. He remembered too how on the big European farms when cattle died of anthrax and the like the corpses that the farmer so carefully buried were invariably dug up and eaten by his labourers, with no apparent ill effects. So he shot nothing.

There was a great deal of wailing from within the village, and the drums, which they had heard for some time throbbed away, loud and monotonous, but no one came out to greet them as was the usual custom, and it was then that the man remembered Sikoti, and felt guilty that the excitements of the past few days had made him forget his death so easily. The man and Robert walked right up to the gate of the village and still no one greeted them, and when they looked in the reason was obvious. The funeral rites and mourning were in full swing, and the noise of wailing and drumming was deafening. The lack of a body did not prevent this, though the man got the feeling that the continuing losses amongst their cattle was a major disaster which modified their grief to some extent. He saw before one hut what must have been Sikoti's family, prostrated on the ground beside a cow's hide on which rested some of the dead man's few pathetic belongings. They seemed to be very genuinely distressed, as were a few others, presumably close relatives or friends. The man saw Mukadi's wife but could not see Mukadi. Having seen several local funerals he knew that most of the people there were mourning but perfunctorily, though they made a lot of noise and show, so that no one could point them out as being poor mourners and therefore possibly involved in some way with the dead man's death. There were too a few almost professional funeral goers, and these had come for the beef and the beer. They made a good show and some of the men had smeared themselves with white clay and ashes and made rather listless charges across the village stabbing away with their spears at imaginary enemies and evil spirits. The drums did the seemingly impossible and got even louder, and presently the hide and the belongings were taken and buried together with some sour milk, porridge and a pipe and tobacco, outside the village. The grave was slowly filled whilst the wife flung herself on it repeatedly. The rest of the villagers went back to slaughter the cattle which Sikoti, in his lifetime, had chosen for just this occasion. Beer began to flow, and as the party got wilder the man and Robert quietly slipped away before the orgy started, for this was an occasion when normal laws governing adultery were suspended. They still had not seen Mukadi.

He appeared next morning as the sky lightened, greeting the man and Robert but offering no explanation as to his whereabouts on the previous day.

The man returned the greetings, adding, "I see you are dressed for a journey. I hope you will not be away long. I have seen that the same disease which is killing the game is killing the cattle, and I have arranged for a friend of mine skilled in these matters to come from the big city to help you. He will be here today."

Mukadi was silent for a while before replying. "You are good to me and my people, Bwana, but in this matter you cannot help, for this is a thing far beyond the understanding of white men and most of us too," and hearing this the man's hopes fell for he realised that witchcraft was being blamed for the disaster.

Mukadi continued "We do not normally have trouble with our cattle which are disease free and used to the hard conditions of the bush. We do not have the need for medicines for them as we do for ourselves, and thus when something like this happens we need to see a diviner."

"You mean a witch doctor?"

"No, no, Bwana, someone quite different. I mean what I say, a diviner, one who can see and reveal secrets that others cannot. They are especially good at revealing the cause of diseases like this. The cure of the disease is not his concern generally. That may need the services of the doctor."

"But the vet is coming and he can tell you what is causing the trouble," said the man, not troubling to add that the vet could probably do little about it.

"Bwana, he will come and tell us with long words we do not understand what he thinks is causing it, and he may even be right according to your ideas, for even we can see the purging and the ulcers which are killing the cattle. But he cannot tell us the root cause."

"What do you mean?"

"The real causes are difficult to find and are remote. Much skill is required in the divining, for the cause will lie in a fault of one or more people. Perhaps someone has broken a taboo, or done some evil thing. Perhaps someone has bewitched the cattle. perhaps ancestral spirits are

After the Funeral

acting directly against us because they are displeased. And if none of these is the cause then it must be by the direct action of the Supreme Being. In fact this is likely in such a big catastrophe as this."

"Yes, I can see how you can think that these things are as you say as far as the cattle are concerned, but not as far as the game is involved," replied the man. "I cannot understand how that can be at all."

"Bwana, there are many things we do not understand, even you white men. But I must leave you as I am going now to see the Diviner."

"Will you be away long? It would be good for you to see my friend when he arrives."

"Who can tell with these matters?" replied the old man. "He lives not far from here in the forest, and I hope to be back when the sun dies this evening. Stay well Bwana. Stay well Robert," and he strode off.

"What do you think," Robert?" said the man as he watched him go.

"Bwana, what I think is of no importance. What is of importance is that whilst you have been talking I have been watching and I can see the dust of Bwana Dick's Land Rover across the burn."

"Well done," said the man. "Put on the kettle," and as he did so the man cursed himself for his lack of vigilance, which he knew could be fatal in the bush. "Be as careless as that when you are amongst the lions and elephant and you won't live long. That's the second time you have been careless in a few days," he thought.

He watched the approach of the Land Rover in a cloud of black dust, and soon his friend drew up at the camping spot and got out with his staff. It was not easy to see which was the white man.

"Rinderpest all right," shouted Dick as he got out. "I've had a look at some of the carcasses on the way here. Now that fat's in the fire. What about some breakfast, Robert?" and as it was prepared the two friends confirmed their plans to go south through the game country to pick up the other vehicle.

Chapter 16

The Diviner

From his hiding place in the trees the diviner's assistant watched the path leading from the villagers into the forest. He was there to spot the approach of any client for his mentor, and then, after memorising any distinguishing features such as clothing, baggage or weapons, to slip off back to the diviner's without being seen. His report gave the diviner an initial advantage over the unsuspecting client.

In spite of his age Mukadi travelled easily and fast, carrying his spear loosely and with a bundle over his shoulder. The watcher spotted and recognised him, and slipped down from his perch and made his way quickly to the diviner's hut, where he told what he had seen.

Mukadi was not long behind him and entered the glade where the diviner lived. Seeing that it was apparently deserted he squatted on his haunches beside the small fire in front of the hut to wait. An apparently disembodied voice boomed from the hut. "I see you, Mukadi. Greetings. I see your spear and I see your bundle. I see the red feathers in your headring, but I am more familiar with Death than you. What do you seek?"

Mukadi laughed and stood up. "Come out of there, Mungabe my old friend. You might convince the youngsters with your tricks, but if you want to convince an old Hunter of your powers you must tell your assistant not to hide where there are masuku leaves, the hunted ones' friends. He made as much noise almost as a rhino as he crackled off through them. And do not speak of my red feathers. I notice that for all your powers you do not wear them, so I do know more about death than you in a practical way. It would be wise to remember it."

The hut door opened and a man of Mukadi's age came out. "Enough, enough, Mukadi," he said, grinning sheepishly. "Let us not quarrel, and I must get a new apprentice."

This was Mungabe. He was dressed in a simple kilt of monkey skins and wore a thick ivory bracelet on his right wrist. His body carried no paint, but glistened with the butter with which he had oiled himself. He wore no charms or talismans, but his hair was almost white, adding to the dignity he already had. He clasped Mukadi's hand in greeting. Mukadi, who in his warrior's way had noted the oily skin, had made a mental note that if it came to fighting he must not try to wrestle, but

The Diviner

spear him immediately. He said "You do not need to put on a show for me. We have known each other too long. If I did not believe in your powers I would not be here, for it is a heavy thing that is troubling me. but first, here is payment," and, opening his bundle he laid out 3 iron hoes, 3 axe heads and a cloth bag containing a pound of black powder, for he knew that Mungabe owned an ancient muzzle loader.

Mungabe's eyes opened wide. This was generous payment indeed, and it was given, as was proper, before it was asked for and with no haggling.

"You are generous, Mukadi, but then it is well known that you are so. But this is high payment, and your problems must be big."

Mukadi came to the point without further ado. "It is the cattle," he said. "They are dying so fast that we shall be hungry as well as ruined. Bad luck is following me where-ever I go, sticking to me like a shadow," and he told of the burning of the grazing, for which he blamed himself, and of the death of Sikoti, and told also of the death of the game, adding at the end "as we know, if the will of the Supreme Being is at work there is nothing any of us can do; but if it is due to some fault of me or my people or due to witchcraft or the evil influence of ancestral spirits, then I must know, so that I can take steps to halt the trouble. I need your help."

The diviner listened throughout without movement or comment. When Mukadi ended his story he shifted on his heels and said, "All this I know. Obviously. My cattle are dying as fast as anyone elses. There are hard times ahead of us all. I think that a thing as big as this can only be due to the will of Leza, the Supreme Being. But you are right. We must be sure it is not due to anything else, for against the other things we can take action."

He called over the shame-faced assistant, and spoke to him, after which he went into the hut and came out carrying a small earthen cooking pot, and whilst he blew the ashes until they were glowing, Mungabe went into the hut, bringing out a small sack, which he opened to reveal small bags inside. Some of these contained pieces of wood or bark, some powders, some roots, and some various kinds of leaves. It was the leaves he was interested in now, and sorting through them he selected a handful of different ones and threw them into the pot, which he pushed into the glowing ashes. Soon a pungent, thick smoke began to curl up from the mouth of the pot, and at this Mungabe went into the hut again and came out carrying a thick curved stick, one end of which was carved into the likeness of a snake's head. This was his divining rod which he maintained could possibly answer some of their problems. Grasping a handful of smouldering leaves he rubbed some over his body and some over the snake's head, and then placed the stick on the ground

White Tail

between Mukadi and himself. Mukadi watched, fascinated and silent, and presently Mungabe said, "I am going to question the stick. If the answer is "no" nothing will happen. If it is "yes" you will see for yourself what will happen," and taking up a small calabash filled with pebbles which he used as a rattle, he began to shake it gently and to chant in a low voice words which Mukadi could not make out. Suddenly he began to ask his questions, and he asked many, but the stick never moved.

He confirmed what they had believed from the start that no taboos had been broken, no evil deeds done, no witchcraft was at work, and no spirits upset.

Mukadi was not very impressed with all this, as all the questions aksed had been phrased for the negative answer, and no movement of the stick was expected, but as he watched Mungabe said suddenly, "Is it all then the will of Leza?" and at this the rod began to move jerkily, the snake's head tapping the ground vigorously. Mukadi's eyes narrowed and his whole being tensed, but he could see quite clearly that in no way was Mungabe touching the stick, and yet it moved, and moved strongly.

"There is our answer," said Mungabe. "are you satisfied now?"

"Yes, I am, and I am glad that it is an act of Leza and that there will be no smelling out of witches or placating of spirits. Come now, old friend. How do you do it.?"

Mungabe was genuinely angry. "I do nothing. The rod is moved by a friendly spirit anxious to help us. Do not mock."

Chastened but still not entirely convinced Mukadi replied, "Perhaps the spirit can help us with my bad luck. What do you think?"

"We can try," and the stick was re-doctored with other leaves. It was much more lively this time in response to the questions, and vigorously asserted that "Yes a person had offended the spirits", and that "Yes, that person was Mukadi", but repeated questions as to how he had offended were fruitless, and as the lives of the Ila were so riddled with rules and taboos of all kinds it was not difficult for them to believe this.

"I accept that I have offended them," said Mukadi, "though I cannot think how. Now let us find out how I am to make restitution."

So the questioning went on, but the snake stick gave no more information and lay motionless.

"What do we do now? I must know how to make amends," said Mukadi.

"Don't be impatient," said Mungabe. "There are other methods I can use. The snake stick has obviously done all it can. and now I shall see what the sacred axe reveals," and he did so, using the axe in the same way as he had used the rod, doctoring it and then questioning it,

The Diviner

but perhaps the method was so similar, for there was no result and no help obtained. "I feared as much," said Mungabe. "Now we must use a different way. Fetch me Kateka, the sacred mortar."

The assistant again disappeared into the hut, emerging this time with an ordinary mortar such as the women used for pounding grain. He washed it carefully, and setting it down on the ground between the two men, filled it with clear water. Mungabe dived into his sack again and pulled out a small bag of powder. This he poured into the water which became inky and opaque as it disolved, and when it was mixed to his satisfaction he hunched over the mortar and shading his eyes with his hands, peered into the murky liquid in the same way as a crystal gazer peers into her crystal ball in Europe. He was silent for some time and then grunted and looked up at Mukadi, who asked him, "Do you see anything?"

"Yes," came the reply, "but I do not understand what I see. I see an animal, which is large and black and difficult to make out. Behind it is something white. I begin to see it more clearly now. It is a large buffalo bull and the thing behind is a white tail!"

"Ridiculous," said Mukadi. "Whoever heard of a buffalo with a white tail?"

"Do not mock, Mukadi. There are many things we do not understand, but the spirits do. This buffalo with the white tail is connected with you. Perhaps it has to do with your bad luck."

"Very well. What do I have to do? Must I find this unlikely buffalo? Must I kill it? What must be done to satisfy the spirits?"

"None of these," was the reply. "I cannot see well, but none of these, and this I cannot understand. But I can see that the day you find the white-tailed one your bad luck will stop for ever. It will not be soon, and you must never stop looking, for even the act of seeking will help alleviate your bad luck." He peered once more into the depths, and then suddenly got up and tipped out the water.

"What did you see?" asked Mukadi. "Something upset you."

"Nothing. I saw nothing. Now go. You have wasted my time enough for one day. Stay well old friend."

Chapter 17

Recovery

Time slipped away. The man and Robert returned to their home. The vet, having done what little he could do, returned to the capital to direct his campaign to save the country's cattle. Mukadi tended the remains of his cattle which he dearly loved, and they slowly began to recover, but only one in ten survived. He brooded over a white tailed buffalo, asking passed strangers if they had seen such an animal until he began to get a reputation for oddness, and his senior wife went as far as to consult Mungabe about him, and he re-assured her.

And on the flats opposite the island where the grass was lush and fresh a small white tailed buffalo and what remained of a once huge herd, slowly recovered too.

PART 3 THE ADULT

Chapter 18

White Tail Grows Up

It was six years since the rinderpest epidemic had swept through the Kavuvu flatlands, devastating the cattle and the game. The remnants of the buffalo herd which the orphaned White Tail joined had made their way slowly and laboriously to the big river with its lush grazing. Many had died from weakness on the way, but there were no new cases and the disease gradually died out.

Recovery had been prolonged and the herd had been very slow to increase in size. The disease had made many cows infertile, and even when a cow did become pregnant there was no guarantee that she would calve, abortion being common. Many bulls too seemed to be sterile, so that the late effects of the disease were almost as bad as the early ones, though not so spectacular.

The old herd bull who had saved White Tail's mother from the lioness was dead. Living he had feared nothing, fighting his way to mastery of the herd, taking the best cows with none to gain say him. He took his responsibilities seriously, guarding the herd well and killing no fewer than six lions in his time. Only the elephant made him give way, and on one epic occasion when he had been drinking at the river he had got between it and a bull hippo, which attached him. They fought an honourable draw, the buffalo carrying a scar on his shoulder for the rest of his days made by his opponent's chisel-like incisors, and the hippo had a raking gash from the buffalo's horns the length of one side, which he carried with him till the day he was killed in a fight with another bull hippo and then torn to pieces by the crocodiles. But the old animal had been helpless against the insidious disease, dying puzzled and uncomprehending, anxious to get to grips with the enemy he could not see. And so the herd lost his strength, his potency and his wisdom, as well as several of his lieutenants who died with him. These had aided him in his guardianship of the herd, even whilst they had waited for a chance to oust him and lead the herd themselves. Only some of the younger bulls and yearlings survived, and eventually the former fought for the cows and the leadership, and a new herd bull emerged, though he was but a shadow of his predecessor. The others waited for the time which they felt was not too distant when they could oust him.

The matriarch too had died, but with less regret than the others. She was old and weary and her wisdom became a burden to her as the herd continued to rely on her. The calves and yearlings which used to please and amuse her with their noisy energy now only irritated her, and her arthritic joints pained her constantly, so that she died quickly and almost gratefully, her vast cunning dying with her. Many other old cows died too, and there was no immediate successor to her.

The effects of the lack of mature leaders became evident soon enough. The predators who waxed fat and numerous on the carrion produced by the epidemic eventually had to hunt again, only to find game scarce. They harried it ceaselessly. The buffalo had neither the physical nor the numerical strength to defend themselves, nor had they the cunning of experienced leaders, and many were taken.

But, in spite of everything, the herd was now, six years later, at last beginning to recover. It was nearly 400 strong, and its sheer size guaranteed protection against enemies. The lions which, after the bounty of carrion produced by the epidemic, had prospered, running in large, well-fed prides with many cubs, now began to feel the pinch. Large prides need large quantities of food, which means hard and constant hunting; but, being by nature lazy and devoid of any family feeling, the older lions were not prepared to do this, and having gorged themselves did not worry about the cubs. These, relying on scraps only, and by now weaned, began to die of starvation, so that many were snapped up by hyaena or cannibalised by other lions. All this led to a gradual lessening of pressure on the buffalo herd, which, benefitting from the good grazing and plenty of water, began to look fat and sleek and healthy again, and the calves became more numerous as the fertility of the herd returned.

*　　　*　　　*

White Tail, now fully grown, was bigger than most of his fellows. Standing five feet at the shoulder he was a formidable mass of powerful muscle. His horns were his pride, very symmetrical and curving downwards before sweeping up again to end in needle-like tips. They were not particularly long, but very thick and heavy, and the bases covered his skull completely where they met over his forehead, forming an impenetrable shield protecting his brain against anything attacking him from the front, which would be a foolhardy thing to do anyway. But they were not purely defensive, their weight making them an efficient battering weapon, whilst the sharp horns slashed mercilessly anything coming within reach. The neck was developed into a mass of knotted muscle capable of carrying the weight of head and horn, and the rest of his frame was in proportion. His hide, when rain-washed, was a dull jet black apart from the white tail which named him. Since the age of about four he had been serving the cows in the herd when he could, fighting for them, sometimes winning and sometimes losing, but the number of times that he lost was getting less and less.

But thoughts of cows and fighting were far from his mind as he stood there on this particular day. He was enjoying himself in spite of the late October heat, for with thirty or so of his fellow bulls he had withdrawn a little way from the main herd for peace and quietness, and they all stood hock deep in dense reeds in a backwater of the Kavuvu. It was very hot and oppresive and they enjoyed the coolness of the water round their legs. Occasionally one of them would leave the cover of the reeds and move to an adjacent mud wallow and roll in the thick sticky mud, until he was plastered with it. The mud served both to cool them and to give relief from the numerous insects which lived amongst their hairs and in the cracks in their hides. The reeds were very dense, thick and matted, and also very tall, so that once amongst them the animals were very well shaded. Egrets and oxpeckers moved amongst and over them, removing insects from their hides.

White Tail decided to go to the wallow and pushed his way through the reeds towards it, his bulk making a tunnel. He stood, just hidden at the edge of the reeds, testing the air and looking and listening carefully. What wind there was blew from behind him and he was uneasy, but all seemed safe, and he stepped from his cover and flopped into the nearby wallow sending up a crowd of irritated egrets, who, however, quickly settled again to their endless task of feeding themselves. The mud was cool. There had been a little rain, but though the clouds built up every day promising a downpour, every evening they dissolved and dispersed, as they would do again today, giving no relief to the parched land.

Chapter 19

Chipimo

Mukadi sat half dozing in the shade of the wide eaves of his hut, but found there was little relief from the sticky October heat on this sultry, airless day. The six years that had passed since the epidemic and the loss of nearly all his cattle had left their mark on him, and his hair was white, as was his little beard, and his figure was more bent, though he still worked hard and took a great interest in his work as headman of the village. His fat dumpy senior wife on the other hand had changed very little, and she was as cheerful and plump as ever as she sat near him, sorting through mealie seeds which she intended the junior wives to plant soon, dry, if necessary, to await the rain.

Mukadi stirred and she glanced at him.

"Let me bring you some water," she said, putting aside her basket.

"Thank you. I would like some or even better some sour milk. It is hotter than ever this year. I can't remember it ever being so hot."

The woman laughed. "You say that every year. It's not true. It is neither hotter nor cooler than last year, but you are a year older and like the heat less. I'll get the water. There's no sour milk, the children have drunk it all".

She returned presently, giving him the water and resuming her task, occasionally flicking out a bad seed which was snatched up eagerly by the chickens round her feet.

"I think that at last we are over the worst," she went on. "The cattle are building up again and the game has recovered, and your bad luck has stopped as far as I can see. Perhaps Mungabe had something to do with it since he passed over to the Spirits."

"Maybe," said Mukadi, and was silent for a while, remembering his friend who had died two years before. Eventually he resumed, "But you know, he was very agitated when he was dying because I had not found the white tailed buffalo. I admit I was thinking about it less and less, but he was emphatic that I should go on with my search, for only when I found it would my run of bad luck end. It had apparently ended as far as I could see, but I had to take notice of what a dying man skilled in his art of divining said."

"You worry too much," she replied. "Look at us, we are well, the cattle are well, the crops are good and the granaries are full. The children are fat. Truly I think the bad luck has gone."

"Perhaps, perhaps; I hope you are right. But he seemed so certain about the buffalo and that I should meet it, even going so far as to give me his muzzle loader before he died, as you know, so that we could meet on more even terms," and he began to day-dream as he sat on his little three-legged stool, remembering the years he had spent after he had consulted his now dead friend, searching for a white tailed buffalo. He had travelled through wild country seldom if ever trodden by men, following many herds and groups, but he never had found the animal he sought. He asked for it at remote villages, and followed rumours into the temporary fishing camps on the Kavuvu. He asked travellers who had come down from the north if they had seen such an animal until everyone in Ila-land knew of his quest, and thought him crazy at the worst or senile at the best, and humoured him, until he learnt to keep his own counsel, speaking only to his senior wife about it. But he never found what he looked for.

He awoke with a start to find that his other two wives had arrived, and the younger was saying to his senior wife, "Mother, the children say that your son Chipimo is coming," and sure enough, when they looked across the village and through the gateway a tall powerful young man was coming towards them. He was very different from the boy of sixteen his father had chastised for making smoke on his first hunting trip. He now exuded confidence as he strode along, and the upper part of his body gleamed with oil and sweat and the muscles of his shoulders rippled as he swung his arms. He wore a kilt of monkey skins and a blanket of lechwe skins was draped toga-wise over one shoulder, and over the other he carried a spear. He was an impressive sight, and obviously a man of consequence. Already he wore one red and one blue feather in his headband. The blue he had earned by driving two lions out of the cattle kraal one night. The red he had earned by waiting up in the moonlight for the same lions to return, when he had killed the one, spearing it to death with his one spear as he held it off with the other.

His father had taught him well and he was now an experienced hunter and likely to follow his father as the acknowledged best in the tribe. He was also a cattle owner and had two wives and four children, much loved by their grand-parents. Since they were not with him now Mukadi knew that he had news of importance to bring, or serious problems to discuss.

"I see you Mother, I see you Father," he said. "It is hot," and he handed each of them a small gift, for he was a good son. His mother hurried to fetch water, milk and porridge for him, together with a piece of dried game meat, and he sat beside his father and ate. Though they all

White Tail

knew that he had business of some sort to discuss, no-one was in a hurry to broach the subject. It would have been impolite to discuss anything while he was eating, and when he had finished and had washed his hands they discussed domestic affairs for some time, the state of the grandchildren, the excellence of the cattle, and other matters of small importance but great interest.

Eventually the son said, "My uncle, Mungabe, now with the spirits, was not a fool."

Mukadi looked up sharply. "We know that well, son. But what makes you say so now?"

Apparently changing the subject Chipimo continued "Travellers from beyond the hills in the north, wild men, Chokwe, stayed and drank beer in our village last night."

Mukadi, who knew that the subject had not been changed, said, "They have come far. They must have had stories to tell of their travels."

"They had. Two nights before they stayed with us they had stayed with the fishermen near the Island, and much beer was drunk. But one of the fishermen who had crossed first to the Island and then to the other bank, the west bank, to poach a reedbuck, was chased by buffalo there."

"Yes, that is more than likely," interjected Mukadi. "He was lucky they did not get him, and he was lucky to avoid the lions; fishermen are a foolish lot and should stick to the river."

"One of the buffalo had a white tail."

There was a crash as the senior wife dropped her bowl, scattering seed around her unheeded, to the delight of the hens, followed by a long silence.

Mukadi stared at his son and said, "You would not joke with me or mock me, my son?"

"You know I would not do that. I tell you as it was told to me. It is third or second hand, but it has been told."

"Quiet," said Mukadi to the three wives who had begun to weep and wail gently. "Let me think." But the women were not to be quieted. "It can only mean trouble and bad luck," said the senior wife.

"No. That is not what Mungabe said. He said that when I found a white tailed buffalo my bad luck would end," and he began to question Chipimo further about his news.

When he had finished he turned to his senior wife. "Enough weeping, and keep the other two quiet. You have plenty to do now to prepare for my journey, for I must go now and find him."

"No!"

The word was spoken quietly but emphatically, and Mukadi looked at his son in amazement, for never before had Chipimo contradicted him.

"No, Father," he continued with respect. "It would be foolish to go on a long journey at your age on the strength of what after all is only the tale of a drunken Chokwe. I will go."

"But that is no use. You cannot take my place. I must meet the buffalo myself."

"I agree, but let me finish. I will go and find him if he is there, and I will take Mudenda our cousin who is a sensible boy, with me. If I am successful I will send him back with the news and he can guide you to where I left him, and you can follow the signs I will leave on the trees and bushes as I follow the buffalo to keep in touch with them."

And that was what they finally decided to do, though they talked the plan over endlessly, and the senior wife had to lend all her weight to Chipimo's decision before Mukadi finally agreed. They had long arguments too about the muzzle loader, until Chipimo reluctantly agreed to take it, though he would have preferred the weapons he was used to. The fact that it had been the diviner's and was a link between him and the white tailed buffalo finally decided him. It could perhaps be possessed of magical properties, and in any case he would have the gun doctored before he left so that it would shoot truly at buffalo, if necessary.

Chapter 20

Death of a Warrior

Hoping to avoid the worst of the heat Chipimo and his young cousin left before it was light, hurrying with long strides across the plain. At first the path was well known, but as they left the villages behind Chipimo was at some pains to ensure that the boy was certain of the way they were going, turning him round frequently so that he could fix in his mind what the land looked like going the other way, and pointing out a peculiar tree or a brilliant bush or an anthill which might serve as landmarks. When there was a bunch of tall grass beside the trail which had somehow escaped both fire and grazers Chipimo would tie a knot in it, making yet another guide line for the boy who, they hoped, would travel back alone. Mudenda was a good pupil and enjoyed what he was learning.

Chipimo wished that he had not brought the muzzle loader. It was heavy, an unfamiliar load and interfered with the rhythm of his walking. He supposed that there might be something in the vague connection between the gun and the dead Mugabe and the white tailed buffalo, if it existed, which might be of significance to the Spirits. It was a nuisance though, but he was glad that the necessary doctoring of the gun had been done. This had been no easy thing in the short time available, for it was not sufficient just to make the gun shoot straight, but to make it shoot only buffalo. The old man who had doctored it had been verbose and slow, but the mention of the dead diviner's name and Mukadi's worries, about which the whole tribe knew, had speeded things up. Or perhaps it was the increase in the fee that Chipimo had offered.

As he left the doctor had said "You are in a hurry Chipimo, son of Mukadi. Why do you hurry? Who knows what you are hurrying to?" and then was gone. But Chipimo was glad it was done. For one thing he had never fired a gun before, though he had been taught to load and prime one, but now that did not matter, the whole business of aiming being in the hands of the Spirits, and not his own, for which he was thankful.

So the two men pressed on, parallel to and some five miles south of the Kavuvu. In the distance they could see the gash in the hills through which the river debouched onto the flats, and on the second evening they arrived there, and slept soundly by the river, with a fire, knowing that the next day would bring them to the buffalo, or at least close to them, if they were still in the area.

*   *   *

They found fish on their night lines next morning, and ate as much as their bellies could hold. They were now living off the land and there was no telling when they would eat again. They wasted no time, eating quickly, and then pushed on and were soon through the gap, scrambling over the rocks which lined it and then crossing the small tributary beyond. This was still dry, and in it, scratching around, were hundreds of guinea fowl, not in one large flock but in pairs mostly, with a few scattered larger groups of presumably bachelors who had been unable to find mates. They barely looked up as they scratched or displayed, for this was the breeding season and love had made them careless and stupid. The men could have caught them probably had they so wished. Leaving the birds behind they came to the plain opposite the island, were the puku lived, and where the fisherman had seen the white tailed buffalo.

By now the sun was half way up the sky, the time of day the Ila called "munza", but it was already hot and promised to get hotter. To the north and east the sky was covered with large black thunderclouds, amongst which they could see the almost continuous lightning, though it was too far away for them to hear. Chipimo decided to forgo a rest, as

Death of a Warrior

there was now some urgency about their task. He did not want to find the buffalo and then have them scatter in the coming rains before his father could reach them. There had been no rain yet here, and the buffalo must be near, dependent as they were on the Kavuvu for water. He planned to look for their spoor and droppings along the river bank, seeking the place where they came to drink. When he found it he would either wait for the herd to return to drink, or follow the spoor to the forest, depending on what time of day it was when he found it. So they walked upstream along the river bank, where the big riverside trees gave them some shade and relief from the appalling heat, scanning the ground carefully for any sign of the animals. They were the only living things moving in the Kavuvu bush.

But in the sky there was movement. About half a mile ahead of them were vultures, one minute half a dozen and the next more than fifty, appearing out of nowhere the way vultures do. They were not circling but dropping down on to a spot on the bank hidden from Chipimo by trees and thickets. He hoped that it was not a lion kill that was bringing them down, as he had no desire to tangle with lions, but he hardly thought that it could be at this time of day. Intrigued, careful, and in no way relaxing their search for spoor, the two men approached the spot and soon they could hear them and see the odd one bounce up into the air above the intervening scrub, only to settle again immediately. Chipimo pushed gently through a thick piece of bush, which gave him both cover and protection, the boy close behind. He parted the last few creepers and branches, peered through, and then relaxed, standing up and laughing.

"Come and see this, Mudenda," he said.

Before them was a strange scene. A large python had surprised a young bush buck, catching it and envelopping it, and had begun to swallow it. The animal's head and neck had already disappeared and the python's upper jaw was half way down its back, and the snake was well on the way to ingesting the whole animal when the vultures spied them. The snake was helpless against them, and though they did not attack it, they set about the buck, pulling and tearing at it so that the snake was not able to swallow it further. Quite suddenly and quickly the python regurgitated the animal, whereupon even more vultures joined in the feast, and though the python struck at them repeatedly he could do them no harm, nor could he stop them, and, accepting the inevitable, he slid away towards the reeds.

The two pressed on, and they began to see some buffalo hoof prints and pats of dung, which soon became very numerous, and they were on the spoor of the herd. It was evident that it was a large one, and that it had come down to the river that morning. Chipimo decided that he might save time by following them rather than waiting for them to return in the evening.

The spoor cut a broad swathe through the bush, and they crossed it to find out how wide it was, to get some idea of the size of the herd. It was big all right, and when they reached the far edge of the tracks they turned towards the forest, but had only gone a little way when Mudenda noticed further signs of buffalo about fifty yards to their right. They went to look more closely and found the spoor of some thirty animals, which Chipimo surmised was a herd of bachelors. What was more important was that the spoor went one way only, and there were no return tracks. It led to a reed bed they could see in the distance in a backwater of the Kavuvu.

"We'll try this first, I think," said Chipimo. "We may be lucky and save a lot of time if the white tailed one is with this lot," and they retraced their steps, following the new trail easily until they could see clearly where it entered the reeds.

"I can't make out much," said Mudenda. "Doesn't look as if there is anything in the reeds."

Chipimo said "Keep quiet and use you eyes. If you look closely you will see egrets fluttering up occasionally. Egrets don't go into reed beds for nothing. The buffalo are in there."

"Good," said Mudenda. "I will be very quiet and you can rely on me to do as I am told."

"Let's start now then. Do you see that tree over there?" said his friend, pointing to a large untidy looking tree with deep green leaves and rather uninteresting creamy flowers.

"Yes, it is a tree I know, a muchenje," replied Mudenda, using the Ila name for an ebony tree.

"Go to it carefully and quietly and get up it and stay there until I tell you to come down."

Mudenda's face fell, but Chipimo went on, "Buffalo in reeds are no light thing. I must go in there alone. You cannot help me in there and I cannot keep an eye on you if I want to see these animals and find out if the white tailed one is there. Do not be disappointed. You will have a good view."

Mudenda knew better than to argue, and was soon up the tree safely wedged in a large fork, from which, as Chipimo predicted, he had a good view of the reeds, which, however, remained impenetrable even from this angle, and he could see nothing except the egrets. He did notice however a wallow next to the read bed, and beyond the mud some thick bushes, towards which his cousin was now crawling with the utmost caution, using every scrap of cover.

* * *

Death of a Warrior

Chipimo was glad to reach the cover. He noted the wallow as he passed it, but was concentrating on not making a noise with the muzzle loader, which was more of a nuisance than ever now that he had to crawl with it. He was not sorry now that he had it though, for he was not looking forward to flushing the buffalo out of the reeds, and he decided to load and prime the gun to be on the safe side. This done, he spied out the reed beds. Apart from an occasional egret he saw nothing, but the snuffling and blowing of large animals could now be heard and the rustling of the reeds they moved, and there was now no doubt that the buffalo were there. He looked without enthusiasm, but without fear, at the reed beds and had made up his mind to move when a sudden cloud of egrets rose fussily, fluttering above the reeds, impatient to settle again, and the reeds opposite the wallow began to move. He froze and was glad that there was no wind as the head of a large buffalo appeared through the reeds, eyes flickering and alert as it sniffed the air with raised muzzle. After a minute or so, which seemed like an hour to Chipimo, the buffalo came forward and, satisfied that all was well flopped awkwardly down into the wallow with a deep snort of contentment, covering itself with the glutinous mud through which it white tail was clearly visible.

Chipimo hissed softly.

It was then that he decided to kill the buffalo. It suddenly occurred to him that perhaps his father only needed to see the white tail. No one had ever said that he must see the white tailed buffalo alive. Chipimo convinced himself that he was right and that all he had to do was to kill the buffalo as it lay helpless in the wallow, cut off the tail and return with it to his father, and, suiting his actions to his thoughts, he slowly and carefully raised the old gun. He made no noise but to his dismay felt a puff of wind at his back, and immediately the buffalo was alert as it caught his scent, and as it dragged itself up from the mud Chipimo pulled the trigger. To his surprise nothing happened, and the buffalo made hurriedly for the reeds as the hunter raised the gun to see what was wrong. It was then that it went off with a loud crash which sent every egret up into the air in alarm, its load passing over the rear of the buffalo as it disappeared into the reeds to safety. Chipimo cursed the gun and the gun doctor. The buffalo was now on guard and possibly angry, and he could hear them milling about in the reeds disturbed by the shot, but they did not come out. It never occurred to him that his task was over and that he had done what he set out to do, find White Tail. He was obsessed with the killing of the animal. Foolish he possibly was, but no one could say he was not brave. Abandoning the gun in disgust he took up his stabbing spear and immediately felt more at ease. He walked to the reeds and entered the tunnel made by the fleeting White Tail.

White Tail

As he entered the milling around ceased and all was quiet. He went very slowly along the dark green path, tense and now sure that the buffalo was just ahead of him. White Tail, standing motionless to the side of the tunnel, having circled round on his spoor, watched him pass and then drove his right, massive horn clean through his chest, killing him instantly, and tossed him viciously high into the air and out of the reeds where he followed and continued to gore him. Several other buffalo joined in, and some following the dead man's scent found the old gun and smashed it before the whole herd turned and crashed off right through the reeds and on the plain beyond, where they snorted and wheeled around for some time in the setting sun, before they finally settled. So Chipimo died, and the rain which now began to fall washed his remains gently before the predators arrived.

Chapter 21

Mudenda as Chameleon

Mudenda screamed. He had watched the buffalo emerge from the reeds, and had seen even before Chipimo that its tail was white. It was placid and not at all menacing. He had watched with amazement and concern the fiasco with the gun and the disappearance of the buffalo back into the reeds, and when his cousin followed into the green gloom he realised that he must have decided to kill the buffalo and was still puzzling the reasoning behind this when the bloody body was tossed out of the reeds. He continued to scream. The buffalo did not look at all placid now as he followed the body out, boring and hooking with his horns, one of which dripped gore, until the bloody bundle was scarcely recognisable as having once been human. Other buffalo emerged and tossed the body, and Mudenda's screams stopped when he saw that the white tailed one was crossing the wallow and making for his tree, and it was with relief that he saw the buffalo go for the gun and toss it and pound it until it was smashed to pieces. Then White Tail turned and went back, gave the body a perfunctory toss and then led the others at a fast trot through the reeds and up the bank on to the plain, stopping in the middle of it half a mile away.

Nauseated at what he had seen the boy was at once horrified, terrified and grief-stricken. The sun was going down and it was now raining steadily, cold adding to his misery. He realised that for safety's

Mudenda as Chameleon

sake he must stay in the tree all night, and before settling shinned down and picked up his axe and two spears, climbed up again, and tied the weapons and himself into a large fork with bark rope, in case he fell asleep. But his cup of horror was not full on this terrible day, for as the shadows lengthened he heard the whooping of hyaenas nearby, and watched in dismay and disgust as they appeared through the reeds and began to eat his dead friend. One of them tore off an arm and trotted with it towards the tree under which it intended to settle and eat it. Mudenda's anger overcame his disgust and as it reached the base of the tree he threw a spear as hard as he could, and truly too, for it pinned the animal firmly to the ground having passed through the back and out of the belly. The hyaena thrashed around trying to bite the stick that was pinning it, and indeed tore itself free and moved off dragging its spilled guts, but death was busy with it and it died after a few steps. Mercifully darkness fell and relieved the boy of the visual horrors, but beneath him he heard the other hyaenas chuckling and giggling insanely as they tore and crunched both the man and their dead fellow. Mudenda wept bitterly from grief and fright, but eventually he fell asleep and dozed fitfully until nearly light, when he woke stiff and cold, and as it got lighter he was able to see neither Chipimo's body nor the hyaena's. The other hyaenas had gone. When he felt at last that it was safe he forced himself to descend, and collected their meagre belongings from their cache. He ate some dried fish and some cold porridge and went to the river to drink, and there the new day brought the first change in his fortunes. A lone Ila was paddling a large canoe full of dried fish downstream, standing in the stern and grunting with the effort, obviously making for the nearest market where he could sell his season's work, fifty miles away. Mudenda called and the fisherman, surprised at seeing a boy alone in dangerous country, dug in his paddle and swung the canoe to the shore.

Greetings were passed and the story of Chipimo's death related, and when Mudenda finished the fisherman agreed to carry him as far as the nearest point on the bank to Mukadi's village. A price was agreed and it said much for the tribal honesty that the fisherman had no doubt that the fare would be paid, even on a boy's word. Settling Mudenda on the dried fish he pushed off, and before they had gone very far the boy was asleep.

He did not sleep long. It had been raining gently off and on, but the sky now darkened as black clouds covered it completely and the thunder crashed around them. They could see the rain coming like a grey curtain towards them, but it was the wind that came before it that was the danger as it gusted and swirled furiously, whipping up the surface of the river into choppy waves which were surprisingly big, and the fisherman lost no time in getting to the safety of the shore, for his canoe, heavily laden and with only an inch or two of freeboard, was in danger of being swamped and sinking. He succeeded safely however, and as he and the boy were pulling the canoe as far as they could up the sand bank he had reached, the rain hit them. The electrical storm was now overhead and was bad enough, but it was the rain, coming in solid sheets of water that physically cowed them as they lay under their inadequate blankets beside the canoe. It went on as hard as ever for a quarter of an hour and was then gone, moving up the river and the sky, which only minutes before seemed as though it would be grey for ever, became blue and the sun shone strongly, so that by the time they had off loaded and dried out the canoe and reloaded it they were dry.

When they arrived Mudenda pointed out his village across the plain in the far distance to the fisherman, and it was agreed that he should call there on his way back to collect his dues and to rest, for it was a hard slog back against the current.

The danger and excitement of the storm and the canoe journey had pushed all thought of Chipimo's tragedy to the back of the boy's mind, but as he set off across the plain it all came back to him, and he was not looking forward to telling the villagers the news. He walked slowly along, oblivious to the lechwe which raised their heads as he passed, curious and careful but not frightened as he walked past them. His footsteps became more reluctant the nearer he got, and he felt like that harbinger of death of the folk lore of his people, the chameleon. But eventually he arrived at the village where the population, having been watching his progress for some time, gathered round Mukadi's hut silent, having seen his face. He greeted his Aunt and Uncle, and before he could go further, Chipimo's mother began to scream hysterically and threw herself on the ground beating her head into the earth in her agony as she instinctively knew the worst.

"The news is bad?" asked Mukadi.

"It is very bad, Uncle."

"He is dead?"

"He is dead. Mungabe was right. There is a white tailed buffalo. It killed your son." And he told the whole sad story, missing out nothing, and weeping as he spoke.

As he finished the villagers began their lamentations and wailing. Only Mukadi spoke.

"Give the boy food," he said to his third wife. "He has travelled far with a heavy burden and has behaved like a man," and then he sat down on his little stool and put his head in his hands and wept.

* * *

So there was another funeral in the village without a corpse, and when the last ox had been eaten and all the beer drunk, and the professional mourners thought that they had put on a good enough show, and the genuine ones began to get used to the fact that Chipimo was gone, Mukadi began to make plans.

Chapter 22

The Fight

The buffalo were restless and upset. After killing the man they had blundered through the reeds after White Tail in a state of excitement up on to the nearby plain. There they had milled around, snorting and blowing, long since abandoned by the egrets who were now in their favourite roosting tree near the island, and disturbing the placid puku. White Tail stood in the middle of them, glad of the rain which was washing the blood and its attendant flies from his right horn, so that the watery gore ran down his chest and shoulder, evoking the man smell again and irritating the buffalo, but gently and gradually the rain removed all traces of the encounter. As the sun set the herd began to settle, disturbed only by the whooping and laughing of the hyaenas beyond the reed bed.

Next morning early they watered again in the river but away from the reeds and by the time they had finished some instinct had decided them to rejoin the main herd, especially as the reeds in which they had lain up the day before were now suspect and a place of possible danger. With this in view they drifted off south.

The main herd was watering downstream, having lost two of its members, feeble and sick old cows, to lions at day break. Eight lions attacked the tail end of the herd that they had followed throughout the night as soon as it was light enough to see, killing easily, gorging, and then watching the hyaenas and jackals as they squabbled with the vultures over the reamins. The herd bull had taken the rest to drink at the river, but he had not gone far as he knew that the lions would not worry them further for some time. As it left the water the herd straggled along, across the plain towards the forest where it would lie up again, the leaders being well on their way before the last stragglers had finished drinking. This did not please the bull and with his helpers he hustled them along to get them into a more compact body, less vulnerable to attack. As they crossed the plain the bachelors rejoined them, to the relief of the bull, and soon they were in the trees and relaxed as far as they ever could relax.

After the herds joined up again White Tail felt a dissatisfaction that he could not understand, and his restlessness persisted, though the life of the herd went on much as usual. The rains became heavy and continuous, which seemed to make him worse, and the streams began to fill and then to flow, slowly at first but soon as raging spates, and it was obvious that the time for the migration away from the river was near. The herd bull was fidgety and anxious to be on the move, as were the older cows, but the combination of an unusual number of calvings and the coming into season of a large number of females delayed things. There were enough cows waiting to be served for the mating to go on reasonably amicably until one morning, White Tail, his natural aggression sharpened by the killing of the man and heightened by the rut, began to mount a willing enough heifer, only to find himself butted furiously in the side and thrown over by the herd bull, which stood menacingly over him, but foolishly did not follow up his advantage. He felt he had done enough to discourage the younger animal, which had never been a threat to him, but he soon realised his error. White Tail decided that this indignity was enough and that it was time for him to make his bid for mastery. He got up, not giving ground as the herd bull expected, and lowered his horns and charged his opponent head on, so that the bosses met with a loud crash, sending the cows and calves hurrying out of the way, but drawing the other bulls to see the fight.

Recovering from his surprise, the herd bull set about the task of battering and bruising White Tail into submission. But he had reckoned without the latter's innate aggressiveness and the inexplicable fury of the younger bull, and found himself in spite of his weight being forced back, and he realised that he might lose. He began to look for a chance to break off in safety. This was not easy. So far they had fought boss to boss, battering and pushing but doing no real harm, the noise of the clashing horns, the grunting and the bellowing sounding far more menacing than they really were. But to break off meant turning, and turning meant exposing an unprotected flank to White Tail. The herd bull knew this, but decided to take the risk, and he broke off receiving the expected sickening thump in the ribs. What he did not expect was that the attack would be kept up, and he had been sure that once he had yielded that would be the end of it, and he had not bargained on the vicious, furious assault which was continued by the other, until at last he was badly gashed from the shoulder to the hip along his left flank, and White Tail let him go. He fled ignominiously, dripping gore, reduced in a few minutes from the herd bull to just another old bull, broken in spirit, who would now live apart from the herd with a few others of his kind,

The Fight

until their strength failed and the lions or hyaenas took them.

White Tail, nostrils dilated and chest heaving with the exertion of the fight, snorted and made his way back to the main body of buffalo, gathering round him favoured females. As he expected, another bull, about his age, made a half-hearted attempt to challenge the new leader, but the fierce immediate reaction discouraged him and he soon gave up. After that there was no challenge to his authority for a year or two. He was now the undisputed Leader.

* * *

Enough time had been wasted with these domestic matters and the sand rivers were rapidly filling and flowing. Lush new grass shone in the clear November sunshine, for the rains had cleansed the atmosphere. It was time for the herd to make their way out to the west to the desert scrub, and back again, utilising the grazing to the full, and White Tail moved them on.

PART 4   THE HERD BULL

Chapter 23

The Fishermen

The tree under which the man was fishing was the only one on a hundred yards of grassy river bank. The grass was cropped short by hippo and was like a lawn, but beyond it, upstream and downstream and on the opposite bank thick forest grew out of rocky broken ground, the trees overhanging the banks and making access to the water difficult. Beside the grass the river formed a large still-looking pool into which the Kavuvu tumbled over rocky cascades and from which it flowed over a series of rapids. The strong current down the centre of the pool carried much debris disturbed by the last rains, even huge trees being swept along, having finally fallen when the bank on which they stood was undermined; but the edges of the pool were placid enough, with gentle currents beneath the bank, in which the fish rested. It was a pool made for fishing and the lone tree from which hung the huge sausage-like fruits which gave it its name might have been put there especially for the benefit of a fisherman. The man was sorry that the tree was not in flower, for the big heavy sprays of maroon flowers it bore were very beautiful and heavily scented, and a favourite food of many birds and animals, and it was a pretty sight in the usually cruel bush to see the monkeys tip the flowers like cups to drink the nectar they contained. The fruits, though were large and hard and ugly, and only the rhinoceroses and the tiny bush squirrels relished them, and, when they were young and fresh, the hippos.

It was mid-day and the man was enjoying the shade, but though the sky was cloudless and the sun directly overhead the heat was not

White Tail

unpleasant, as it was June, near enough mid-winter. He had been fishing since early morning, alone and happy, and a rope tied to a branch of the tree led to a nearly full keep net, the fat bream shimmering as they struggled in their watery prison. He was a patient fisherman and had fished the pool with care and concentration, but now his rod rested slackly in his hand and the line swung in the current, his own fishing forgotten as he watched two fishermen far more skilled than he would ever be. When he first saw the two otters drifting down with the current he had thought that they were small logs, but then he saw that they were floating on their backs, each holding a big bream on its chest which it was eating the way a man eats a maize cob, stripping the flesh from the bones, and finally discarding the carcasses as they reached the tail of the pool. He next saw them at the head of the pool, again, each with another fish, drifting and eating. Four times they did the trip down and up the pool, eating a good eight pounds of fish each in the process, and finally the man saw them on the rocks at the tail of the pool grooming and cleaning themselves as they sat on their haunches, sleek and content and for all the worlds like a couple of cats. The man resumed the fishing which had occupied him for the past three days. He was staying at the camp of a friend, a Game Ranger, whose staff were delighted with the unexpected bounty of fish, whilst he waited for Robert.

Normally he and Robert travelled everywhere together in the bush, but the offer of a lift in a light aircraft to the camp, which, thirty miles upstream from the Island, was the starting point of the man's next walk, had prevented this. Neither persuasion nor threats could induce Robert to get into the plane. A man's place was on the ground and he admitted he was afraid, which was saying something from one who had stood shoulder to shoulder with his master to take the charge of a wounded lion abandoned to its misery by some 'sportsman', relaxing only when the animal lay dead where the man had dropped it, a few yards in front of them. No, he would get there in three days' time he said, and there was no arguing. How he was going to travel three hundred miles in three days the man did not ask, but never doubted that Robert would be there as promised.

Fifty yards or so behind the man, almost hidden by grass and reeds, was a small muddy pool. In another month it would be dry, but now it held many birds, all by now accustomed to the presence of the man. There were many teal and a scattering of sacred ibises, busily probing with their long curved bills, intent, occupied and careless, their startling black and white plumage making them look like long-nosed cassocked and surpliced choirboys. Near them were their apparently less beautiful drab-lookiong brown cousins the hadeda ibises, just a pair, but when the sunlight caught their wings the irridescent flash was truly

The Fishermen

beautiful and a thing to be remembered. These two were much more alert than their gaudier relatives, and when the man heard them take off, giving their raucous but not unmusical cries, he knew that something had alarmed them, and he watched them fly upstream calling continuously and alerting every living thing in the bush. They disturbed the teal which rose in a flurry of wings silent at first, and then as they gained height and circled, whistling away, a sound that brought joy to the man's heart. He realised that the disturbance was probably due to the arrival of Robert, and sure enough after a minute or two he glanced over his shoulder to see his servant settling quietly beside him.

"I see you, Bwana. The Game Guards told me you were here. Are you all right?" said Robert, who was certain that the man could not be without him there to look after him.

"I see you Robert. Yes I'm fine. What about you? You must be tired with the journey."

Robert grinned. "I was lucky. I met a friend with a fish lorry, and he brought me all the way to the camp. He is going on further, to the big river." By this he meant the Zambesi. "I slept most of the way."

"Good," said the man, knowing what the lorry would be like and what the track that passed for a road was like and wondering how on earth it had got so far, let alone be able to do another two hundred miles over roads which got worse, if that were possible. "We will leave first thing tomorrow. Take the fish and dish it out. Keep some for yourself."

* * *

All being well it would take them three days' easy walking to reach the Island, where they would rest and fish, but nevertheless they would start early, for in the bush one never knew what might hold them up, perhaps elephant unwilling to move, perhaps a bush fire, but very often something. Besides the man was of an inquisitive turn of mind and moved slowly when some unusual flower or tree or insect or animal held his attention. There was always something new. Once he had seen a buffalo with a white tail. After the Island they would walk across the new dry flood plains to Mukadi's, to greet him and commiserate with him on the loss of his son, whom the man remembered as a boy. He had heard various versions of the story of his death, and wanted to hear the true one.

Chapter 24

The Rains

It was May and the last of the rains was coming down in torrents, its steady drumming shutting out even the howling of the wind which came with it, bending the tall palms like reeds and uprooting dead and diseased trees, and even healthy ones in its fury. Only the rolling and crashing of the thunder could be heard over the hammering of the raindrops on leaves and grass and wood. Though it was mid-day it was dark, a dull greyness relieved only by repeated flashes of lightning. The huge grey elephants of all the animals seemed to be the only one indifferent to the storm, the rain pouring off their sides in great sheets, forming a curtain through which the calves peered in fright from under their mothers bellies at the strange wet world outside. They were right to be frightened, for some of them would die because of this rain, first sticking in some mud hole from which neither they nor the rest of the herd could extricate them, and then slowly sinking, enfeebled by their struggles, into a suffocating, slimy death. The rhino, the buffalo and the larger antelopes such as the kudu and roan were not much worried by the storm as they stood, backs to the wind, waiting patiently for its passing, but the smaller antelopes were frightened, and sometimes panic-stricken, as the ground softened beneath their feet and walking became difficult. Some animals, the earth dwellers, made for their burrows which they had usually found abandoned by the antbear which had made them. These were the honey badgers, the porcupines, the warthog and their like and they at first were secure and dry, but as the storm went on they became more and more worried as the water first threatened to flood their refuges and then actually did so in many cases, driving out the inhabitants if they were lucky, and if they were not, or were young or feeble, drowning them, for only the longest and best engineered burrows with several branches were secure against this danger. There was no sign of any bird. Those that had a safe nest or refuge in a deep hole in a tree had long since retreated there, but most birds had seen the storm coming and had fled before or round it to a dry place until it was past. Monkeys and baboons sat huddled, miserable and resigned under trees which gave them little shelter, and they too waited philosophically until the storm passed. All normal life in the animal world seemed to be in a state of suspension.

The Rains

With disconcerting suddenness the rain tailed off and stopped, and the sky lightened. The turbulance of the wind died down and a weak watery-looking sun appeared, and in another few minutes the sky was a brilliant blue and the sun beat down on the wet world beneath it, which began gently to steam. The wind shook leaves, relieving trees of the weight of water that was bowing them down as millions of tiny drops of water fell to the already sodden ground in showers which glistened and sparkled with rare beauty as the sun caught them. Vapour rose from the backs of the antelopes hanging wraith-like above them so that they moved like ghosts across the plain, slowly at first until some young frivolous member of the group rejoicing in the warm sun and refreshed by the rain kicked up its heels and skittered about for a second or two, infecting others with its feeling of well-being until they were all skipping and frolicking, but only briefly. They stopped as though ashamed at this unseemly display of high spirits, walking sedately along until the irresistible urge to gambol returned. The birds began to appear again, the barbets and woodpeckers emerging dry and superior from their holes, and slowly the bird talk started again, tentatively at first but soon reaching its normal tinkling, chattering level.

* * *

At the first sign of the storm White Tail had moved the herd into a dense thicket spread between two watercourses, big enought for the whole herd to be hidden within it and dense enough to keep off at least some of the rain. He was glad of the deluge, for the rains, which were about to end, had been very poor generally and this spelt danger for the buffalo. Already on their return circuit they were nearer to the Kavuvu than was comfortable for this time of the year, and some instinct told White Tail this. The tributaries and pools were drying up rapidly. This was a cause for concern because though the herd would never be without water as the Kavuvu never ran dry, fed as it was near its source by the heavier more prolonged rains at the southern edge of the Great Congo forests, grazing was another matter. The sooner they were forced back to the river for water the sooner would the lush riverine pastures be denuded as the dry months passed, and the necessary trek of the buffalo from water to grass would become longer and longer, more exhausting and less rewarding in food, until disaster would follow; the weaker and younger would die, emaciated and dehydrated, whilst the survivors gazed anxiously through dull glazed eyes at the sky for the rains, which, if they were early enough, would save them.

These thoughts were in White Tail's mind as he endured the storm, willing it to go on, knowing as he did that at this time of the year it must be the last or nearly the last they would have that season. The herd stood still around him, and as no flies could endure the wet even their tails had for a short time stopped swishing and their heads tossing, and the usual snorting and blowing and snuffing accompanying any herd of cattle went unheard in the constant drumming of the rain and rolling of the thunder. They waited patiently for the rain to end, and when it did they were glad to leave the thicket and stream out on to the grass lands, steaming gently in the sun, where they were soon joined by their attendant egrets which had re-appeared from whatever place of shelter they had found in the storm, flighting in in a fussy agitated crowd. The oxpeckers, those seekers out of ticks, had on the other hand not deserted their hosts, but had stayed with them in the thickets, moving under their bellies for shelter, so that their life's work went on without interruption.

* * *

The lion was in his fifth year, powerful, muscular and thick-set. His two companions were a year younger, and also formidable, but without the quiet menace of their leader. All were fit and well fed, having followed the herd on its migration, killing the unwary. Now they had not fed for three days, and the leader had intended to kill during the coming night, but the rain altered his plans, for the herd, bemused and disorientated by the fury and noise of the storm, emerged from the thicket carelessly. Seizing their chance the lions quickly killed a cow apparently foolish enough to wander away from the rest. In fact they may have been doing her a kindness because a week before, licking a large ant hill for the salt it held she had disturbed a spitting cobra, which, with sickening accuracy, had ejected its venom into her eyes, almost maddening her with pain, and then, later, when the pain subsided, leaving her almost blind, groping along after the herd by scent and hearing, stumbling into her fellows and upsetting them. Be that as it may she was now dead, and as soon as the lions were sure of no retribution, they moved in and gorged themselves. The hyaenas following the lions were glad to see them kill for they too had had no feast for three days, killing only several game birds and some small mammals, and a monitor lizard, well over six feet long and who provided only a snack for the pack. Their greed and hunger led to their downfall. They could hardly wait for the lions to finish before they moved in, and this did not please the lions who had lain down replete a short distance away. One of the younger lions was deputed to chase off the predators, making a few rushes out to the kill, scattering the vultures and the hyaenas, but no sooner had the lion returned to his couch in the long grass than the feasters returned. This repeated and useless performance irritated the large lion beyond measure and soon he was crouching, tense and alert, ready to move. When he did it was no mock

The Rains

attack and he moved as fast as only a lion can move over a short distance, catching the leader of the pack, who was expecting only a token charge, unawares, killing him with hardly a struggle, though the hyaena, giving a final desperate snap as he died, removed the last six inches of the lion's tail, black tuft and all, infuriating the lion who caught and killed another of the scattering pack. He was fortunate that he could reach the wound to lick it, and it eventually healed well, but the short-tailed lion became in time notorious amongst the poachers and game guards and nature lovers who passed through his territory not only for his short tail but for his temper, which was not uncertain but uniformly bad, making him something of a menace. He became known as Shakalongo after the name of the plain where he lost his tail.

* * *

The man had not enjoyed his walk very much so far, the grass being high except on the dambos and these were flooded, so he had not seen much game. The grass reached well above his head and was not pleasant to walk through, restricting vision, and except at mid day showering him with drops of cold water. In spite of the poor rains the river was in full flood and the rocky islands dotted along its length were invisible beneath the swirling surface, which was not surprising as it had risen some twenty feet above its dry season level inundating and refreshing the riverside plains as well as the islands, causing the man to make long detours. There was no question of a peaceful stroll along the bank for it too was submerged. The flood was powerful, tearing away great rafts of vegetation and undermining and collapsing at last river-side trees which had been living precariously for the past few years, their roots exposed, a little more unstable each year, until the end came and the whole tree crashed down and was swept away. Not all the debris was vegetable. Bloated corpses of animals caught on pieces of land which first became cut off by the water and then inundated, swept along until they finally jammed in some obstruction and were welcomed by the crocodiles. The main stream could be made out by the rapidly moving floating rubbish and dirty looking foam on its surface. So, between the water and the long grass the man had a difficult march. Practically all he had seen were elephant and hippo, well away from the river not at all inconvenienced by the conditions, and enjoying the rich wallowing there for them on the flooded plains. Nor had he been able to fish. The fish spread over the plains, but it was impossible to catch them, though Robert had speared a couple of fat barbel as they moved over the wet grass making for somewhere to spawn, but they were not the best eating and were too heavy for Robert to carry them far, so they were left, to be found later by a pair of fish eagles who were not averse to carrion, and who with difficulty half dragged, half carried them to a drier spot to enjoy, and there they were joined by other eagles before all the birds were driven off by some hyaenas which made very short work of the remains. The good fishing would come in a few weeks' time when the water on the plains would stream back through numerous channels into the main river. As soon as part of the bank was exposed the man and others like him would seek out a dry bit at the edge of one of these channels to catch the bream congregated at its mouth to reap the benefit of the food being swept in from the rapidly drying plain. But at present there was nothing. This was the fourth day of their walk and, emerging sodden from a patch of long grass, Robert said "I can see the palm trees on the Island, Bwana, and the place where the river goes through the hills."

"Good," said the man. "I'm not sorry." He was getting a bit tired of the wet and his knee was aching which always made his curiosity about this land wear thin when if got bad enough. "But I don't think we shall be able to get on it, nor will we be able to cross the tributary where the Kavuvu turns to the East."

"True, Bwana. There is a good place to cross it two miles upstream."

The man took a compass bearing on the still invisible crossing place and was not surprised to see Robert already walking by instinct almost exactly on the line it indicated. As they passed near the Island they could see that it was almost submerged. Only the palms at the highest point of it had their feet dry. The huge acacias had water half way up their trunks, and they could see plenty of large geese roosting in the enormous branches.

Eventually they crossed the tributary and followed it almost to the main river, but not quite, moving away from it and up to the top of the hills overlooking it as it turned, and there they rested. They could see the sodden landscape through which they had walked, and felt satisfaction at the distance they had come. They drank tea in the evening light and watched the Kavuvu rush with irresistable force through the gap and be absorbed on to the huge flood plain to the east which stretched away like a huge inland sea. In the very far distance on the tree line they could see Mukadi's village.

Chapter 25

Hints of Danger

The walking was easier once the man and Robert had passed through the gap, though they had to skirt the floods and keep to the tree line, only occasionally being able to take a short cut across a stretch of plain from which the water had already drained. The nearer they got to Mukadi's the shorter and less obstructive became the grass, for the cattle were near the villages at this time of year, cropping it down as hard as they were able, relishing the abundance whilst it lasted, remembering the hunger the dry season could bring. They were fat and sleek. The two men were walking fast now, delaying only to return greetings which were offered at each group of huts as they passed, and they could see Mukadi's clearly now, almost surrounded by water. A large tarpaulin covering a bulky shape at the entrance to the village told them that the vehicle had arrived, which was a relief. The driver had done very well indeed to get it as far as this considering the state of the going.

They passed the Land Rover and entered the village going straight to Mukadi's hut, directly opposite them, outside which he was squatting and sharpening a spear.

"I see you, old friend," said the man, speaking first as courtesy demanded.

"I see you, Bwana," was the reply.

"I see you, Father," added Robert.

"I see you Robert," said Mukadi, and continued, "You are welcome here as always." This was to indicate that he was accepted in spite of not being an Ila.

As these greetings were being passed the man was horrified to see the change in Mukadi, but was careful to conceal his feelings. The old man was thin and bent and his muscles, strong and wiry, stood out like cords; he was lean, stripped of every superfluous ounce of fat, but not emaciated. His hair, still plentiful, was snow-white, crisp and frizzy, sitting closely on his head like a white skull cap. He had no beard, unlike most men of his age, and it could be seen that his face was deeply and profusely lined, and that the eyes, whilst still bright and alert, seemed infinitely sad.

Unlike the man, Robert had no such fine feelings.

"I am sad to see that you have aged, Father," he said politely. "You must take good care of yourself."

Mukadi looked up at him quizzically with his sad eyes which showed a spark of anger, and he stood up, balancing the spear he had been sharpening in his right hand and then suddenly flung it at a post some twenty paces away, into which it buried itself, not even quivering, but splitting the pole from top to bottom.

"When you are my age Robert, I hope you can do that."

The man hastily intervened, and tactically suggested that Robert should find the driver, and get ready for the next stage of the journey.

"Leave him, Bwana," said Mukadi. "He is young and means no wrong. The driver is at the next village and I will send for him." He grinned. "Eat food, Robert, before you start telling people I am inhospitable as well as old. I am not angry with you." But the man knew he had been glad of the intervention.

"Sit down," continued the old man. "I am old and sad as you see, but I am strong and well."

He called for his senior wife, who greeted the visitors, and asked her for food and drink.

"I need to be fit," he went on, "I am not sharpening my spears for nothing. In October there will be the first Chila since the disease killed all the game and cattle. I am preparing for it."

The man looked up from his food sharply. "The Chila," he exclaimed. "What on earth do you want with the Chila at your age?"

The Chila was the annual buffalo hunt of the Ila people, during which all men of warrior age pitted themselves against the buffalo herds, which were driven towards them by other members of the tribe by noisy drumming and by fire, large areas of the plains being set alight for this purpose. It was a time for a man to prove himself, and many buffalo were killed in the hazy, smoky confusion. The tribesmen did not escape unscathed either. Some were killed and many injured, often seriously, every year. The tribe gorged itself on the fresh meat, and any surplus was sun-dried for use later. Thus the buffalo were moved and thinned out, probably a good thing, and the ever-present problem of food was relieved for a while. The tribe also held a lechwe chila, but this was a tame affair, the small delicate antelope being hunted down with dogs, and no kudos attached to the hunters.

"You may well ask," was the reply. "This is when I miss Chipimo."

"I grieved for you when I heard that he was dead," said the man. "I heard various stories about how it happened."

"You remember him, Bwana. He was always foolhardy. Remember how I chastised him when he made the smoke all those years ago when we were poaching. Well, he did not change and was always impetuous,

Hints of Danger

though a fine man and a good hunter," and then he told the man the story of the white-tailed buffalo and his son's death.

"So you see," he continued, "the white-tailed buffalo exists, and as you know I must find it before my bad luck stops. And now not only must I find it but I must kill it, for I have a son to avenge."

"All this I understand," said the man. "What I do not see is what the chila has to do with it."

"It is in my bones, Bwana, that because of the poor rains that there will be a huge congregation of buffalo by October on the plains near the river, thousands perhaps, certainly hundreds, and they will be trapped for the chila. Amongst them I know that there will be the white-tailed one, and I will find him and my bad luck will end."

"You are wrong, old friend," said the man. "The chilas are for younger men with something to prove. You have nothing to prove. All know of your valour. We are not blind. We can see the red feathers."

"You are right, Master. This old one is an old fool," said the senior wife who had been listening to all this. "Already I have lost my only son, and if this man has his foolish way I shall lose him too, and shall die neglected and alone." Turning to Mukadi she continued "Listen to a man who speaks sense and forget your pride. Go to the chila if you must and look for the white-tailed one, but do not take part, and let there be no killing. Robert was right. You are too old."

"You saw me throw the spear, woman. Was there anything old and feeble about that?"

"No," she replied, "but it is not your strength that is in question, or your skill, but your speed and agility."

"At my age I need neither. I am not going to dodge, turn or run," at which the old woman threw up her arms in despair and wept, rocking backwards and forwards on her stool in her misery.

"She is right, Mukadi," said the man.

"Maybe, maybe," he replied, "for she is wise and is as my right arm to me, and my comfort, but there are other reasons, my friend, which concern my people."

"What can they be?"

After a short reflective silence the old Ila said, "It is a shameful thing. The buffalo will be there in thousands, perhaps. In any case there will be many. Attending the chila to hunt them there will be — Guess."

"A couple of hundred?"

"About a dozen, all about my age, all as stiff and slow as me, more fitted to dozing round the fire and drinking beer than hunting. But what can we do? To the shame of my tribe the young men will not take part. They have no use for tradition, and say openly and without shame that it is dangerous and foolish, admitting their cowardice, strutting in front of the young girls as though they were worth something. Even these they do not court in the old way, preferring the ways of the missionaries," and here he spat on the ground in contempt, whether for the young men or the missionaries or both the man could not tell. "Why," continued the old man, "some of the boys cannot even milk. Can you imagine that? An Ila who cannot milk," and he hung his head in shame and sorrow, weeping for himself, his people, and his dead son.

The man's heart was full too, because he knew now that Mukadi must go to the chila. His honour was at stake. In his fighting days he had had to make similar decisions. He put one hand on the old man's shoulder, and his other arm round the senior wife's shoulder.

"Mother," he said, "he must go. If he did not he would not be the man you married. Stay well Mother, stay well old friend," and with sadness he picked up his cromach and rifle and made for the vehicle where the silent Robert waited, for he too had heard the exchanges.

"Let's move," said the man to the driver.

Chapter 26

The D.C.

"Back to the Government Boma, Bwana?" asked the driver, using the name universally used in this part of Africa for a government township in the bush.

"No, I want to go and see the Senior Chief at the big village," replied the man. "If we keep to the forest we should be able to get there without getting stuck. Something has cropped up and he may be able to help."

The Land Rover jolted and bumped through the trees, weaving in and out between them so that the driver's arms ached, a wheel dropping occasionally into an antbear hole the driver had seen too late, and quite often they had to back up to work their way round some obstacle. But at the expense of sore backs they got on well and eventually emerged from the trees at the edge of a vast plain. It was about a mile across and stretched away to their left further than they could see, for what the man knew was ten miles. The wind rippled across the tops of the rank, yellow grass, over which they could see at the other side the huge circular hut which was the Chief's. The man swung his glasses to the left up the plain and could make out two miles away on the other side a large herd of buffalo, moving back into the forest, and, though he did not know it,

The D.C.

amongst them was White Tail. The plain was much drier than they had thought and they crossed without difficulty.

"Very dry, Robert," said the man.

"Sure, Bwana. It is a bad thing. The people and the cattle will suffer this year."

"It's helping us now anyway," said the man philosophically, and the driver, who was picking his way carefully forwards, nodded in agreement. At the very middle of the plain where the grass was short, and where the main run off had been were three lions and a dead buffalo cow.

"Stop, switch off, keep still and keep quiet," whispered the man. "Let's watch."

A very large male lion lay near the carcass fifty yards from them and two younger males were feeding. All three looked steadily at the vehicle for a few minutes and then the younger ones resumed feeding whilst the old one rested his head on his paws. But not for long. After a minute or two he stood up and without warning rushed at his two companions, cuffing them both and then resuming his rest.

"Very odd," said the man, "but it's late. Let's get on. Did you notice that the end of his tail was missing? That may account for his bad temper. Off we go. We shall have to sleep at the Chief's as it is."

The driver started up and moved off, and as the lions lifted their heads curiously at the noise, he stopped again immediately.

"There is a puncture, Bwana, left rear wheel I think. Must have picked up a big thorn as we passed through the thorn trees back there."

The prospect of mending it close to the lions was not pleasant, but the man readied the big rifle and Robert and the driver got out the spare and the huge lorry jack, and soon had the offending wheel off. It was then that the big lion decided to lend some excitement to the proceedings. The man could see that he was becoming irritated, lashing his stump of a tail back and forth, and suddenly he came. The man was ready and as he aimed he subconsciously marvelled as he had done in the past at the speed of the charge. The bullet crashed inches over the lion's head, and was enough to stop him.

"Coward," thought the man. "If you had been a buffalo you would not have stopped until one of us was dead."

All three slunk off resentfully and the man relaxed his pressure on the second trigger.

"Get on with the puncture," he said, "and let's get to the village," laughing as the two servants emerged from under the vehicle. They finished the job very quickly!

* * *

White Tail

The man had rummaged in the back of the Land Rover until he found a sack of sugar and one of salt for the Chief, and with due regard for local protocol handed them over on reaching the Chief's house. Courtesies were exchanged, and having received permission to camp in the village, the man dismissed his servants and settled down to talk with the Chief. Beer and food were brought and eventually after many enquiries about cattle and the health of the man and his family the Chief said, "You made a lot of noise with the big rifle today."

The man explained what had happened.

"That is the lion we call Shakalongo. He is a bad one all right. I'll be glad when the buffalo move off and take the lions with them. Why didn't you kill him? You will have to one day."

The man prevaricated, being too tired for a discussion on the rights and wrongs of conservation, which in any case would have been incomprehensible and foolish in the Chief's eyes. A nuisance was a nuisance in his view, and nuisances were removed if at all possible.

As they ate more small talk ensued, and then, getting tired and judging that the preliminaries had gone on long enough the man said "I was at Mukadi's today."

"Ah, Mukadi," said the Chief. "A great hunter carrying a great curse which brings him bad luck. Did you know that the white-tailed one is with the buffalo you saw this evening?"

"No," said the man. "No, I did not know that. How did you know about him?"

"He killed Chipimo, remember. We all know about him all right."

"Mukadi says he will kill him at the Chila."

"I hope so," said the Chief. "He wants badly to avenge his son, I know."

The man then told the Chief how Mukadi had aged, and how he feared for him, and how determined he was to take part in the chila, and how disgusted he was with the young men. He went on, "I understand about the honour of the tribe, but these twelve old ones will be killed or crippled needlessly. You are the Chief and you have the power to stop it. Let me carry you in the car to the District Commissioner so that you can talk with him and stop it. I fear greatly for these twelve brave but foolish old men."

The Chief smiled sadly and wearily.

"All you say is quite true, but all Mukadi said was true too. I also an ashamed of the young men. But," and here he looked the man full in the face, "I am one of the foolish twelve. How could I call it off and face my people afterwards?"

The man nodded resignedly, and shook the Chief by the hand.

"You will be remembered as great warriors," he said, and, pleading

The D.C.

tiredness, made his way to his sleeping bag, and had barely time to think of all that had happened that day before he was asleep, and the next thing he remembered was Robert squeezing his shoulder gently and saying "Tea, Bwana. It is dawn."

* * *

Some time during the night, Robert and the driver had repaired the puncture, finding the cause to be, as they expected, an acacia thorn. They had filled the vehicle and checked it over and now were sitting in the cold morning air drinking tea, reluctant to leave the warmth of their fire.

"They are saying that a Game Department Land Rover crossed the top end of the flats from the Mission on the way to the Boma, Bwana," said the driver.

"Are you sure?"

"The villagers are sure," replied the driver.

"In that case we will go to the Mission and check. I find it hard to believe though," said the man. "Let's go and see."

Going this way meant that they did not have to recross the plain where they had seen the lions, but took a line through the forest on this side of it, following a footpath. They had not been long on their way when they found themselves amongst the buffalo. There were about five hundred of them as far as the man could judge, but in the trees it was difficult to make even a rough guess. They were quite docile, milling around peacefully, lowing and snorting, eyeing the vehicle with curiosity. The driver began to edge between them and they moved slowly out of the way as it suited them, for all the world like cattle in a country lane. Just as they cleared them Robert spotted White Tail, and the man was impressed with his size and was glad to see him again. He was equally unaggressive, coming forward towards them, stopping only a few yards away, so that the man again indulged his fancy that the animal recognised him.

They soon arrived at the Mission, a lonely spot with its school, dispensary and church. The Missionary and his wife were polite enough, but were believers in the perverse precept that it is better to receive than to give, and offered them no refreshment. Being, like most of their tribe, professional beggars of rare skill, they managed to let the man know that they were short of this and that, and he, as usual, did what he could for them from his own stores, despising himself as he did so. They confirmed that the Game Department Land Rover had gone through a week ago. The man expressed surprise at this and the missionary agreed that it was early, but it was a fact. He presumed it had got through anyway, for it had not returned.

Robert and the driver had been watching this exchange with

undisguised contempt, regarding missionaries as parasites, and more than that, unkind people who would not give medical treatment unless the unfortunate sick person attended a service either before or after treatment. All three were glad to get away from the place.

The Mission was on the edge of the flats, and when they reached them they could be seen to be covered with water and resembled a large lake. The water was dotted with anthills, and from these they reckoned that the water was only a foot or so deep.

"It looks possible," said the man. "Have you got the old shoe boxes?" and was glad when the driver produced them. Together they tied them over the engine, so that the water which would be thrown up by the fan and which would bounce off the underside of the bonnet cover would not wet the plugs and immobilise the vehicle.

Robert had not been idle. He had walked into the water and reported that it was indeed only about a foot deep and that the bottom was fairly firm, with only a couple of inches of mud covering it.

"I'll drive," said the man, "then you won't get the blame if we get stuck", grinning at the driver. Getting into four-wheel drive and low reduction gear they ground their way without any real difficulty across the water on a compass bearing, suffering occasionally when they passed over an area where the elephant had been and made foot deep holes in the muddy bottom, and keeping their fingers crossed where the water was over two feet deep and flowed through the cab. The man stopped for nothing, not even to inspect the Game Department Land Rover they found abandoned half way across, and where it would remain until the waters went down. He was exhausted when they got to the forest on the other side and glad to hand over to the driver again. Two hours later they arrived at the Boma.

* * *

The D.C. was just leaving his office for lunch when the man drew up. He was a large burly man, well over six feet, but softly spoken. He ruled the district firmly but fairly and was well liked by the Ila. He was delighted to see the man and offered him lunch which was accepted, for the two were old friends. Typically, the D.C. called an orderly and asked him to fix Robert and the driver up with food.

"Better arrange for somewhere for them to sleep," he added. "You will stay the night, won't you?", he said to the man; and without waiting for a reply advised Robert to keep his hands off his staff's wives, and led the way to his house.

The man was happy to stay the night. On lonely out-stations with perhaps twelve Europeans all told, including wives, it would have been churlish to refuse, for visitors were a rare treat to be enjoyed by all.

The D.C.

"Good," said the D.C. "I'll get Mary to ask everyone in for dinner this evening. Did you have a good trip? You're crazy to walk at this time of year. Tell me all about it," and then he added "No, don't. A drink first and then you can tell me about it in comfort.

The D.C.'s wife was equally glad to see the man, and, like most of her kind, was not at all perturbed by the thought of twelve for dinner at short notice.

The man took his gin to the shower and after he had changed they had lunch, after which he fell asleep in a chair over his coffee, awakening shamefacedly at tea-time to find Mary pouring tea, and brushing aside his apologies.

"I was glad you were out of my way; Cook and I had a fair bit to do. John won't be long. Everyone can come, by the way, and you will have to excuse me again. I'm still a bit pushed. Anyway, here is John, so you won't be on your own."

"Well," said the D.C. when the first cup of tea had gone down. "How was the trip? Leg O.K.?"

"It was all right," said the man. "Not much fun at this time of year as you say. But I'm glad I've done it," and he told him of the journey.

He went on "Remember Mukadi?"

The D.C. nodded.

"I saw him yesterday before I went on to the Chief's where I stayed last night."

"Yes, I know," replied the D.C., but the man was not surprised any longer at his friend's intelligence service. "How was Mukadi?"

"Fit enough, I suppose. Looking a lot older and not very spritely, but he's getting on of course. You know he has this thing about a white-tailed buffalo?"

The D.C. nodded again.

"I'll never understand these people and their witchcraft. Did you know the buffalo exists?"

The D.C. looked up in interest. "I've heard things," he said cautiously.

"Well it does. I've seen it several times. I first saw it when it was a calf and I've seen it a few times since. The last time was early this morning."

"I'm glad to know," said the D.C., accepting the fact without question.

"Well Mukadi intends to take part in the chila. He believes that the white-tailed buffalo will be there and that he will kill it and his bad luck will end. Damned witchcraft. I told him he was too old and he went on about the young men and the tribal honour, and how there were only twelve old men to take part now."

"I know; I'm worried about it."

The man went on. "When I was unable to persuade him to give up the idea I went to the Chief and asked him to call it off, or at least come here with me to discuss it with you. Turns out he is one of the twelve and won't budge."

The D.C. smiled sourly. "So you have come to twist my arm?"

The man did not deny it."Yes, I have. These old boys will be killed or maimed as sure as eggs are eggs. What do you think?"

"It's got to go on," and raising his hand to stop the man's protest he added, "Half a jiffy. I agree with you all the way, but the powers that be have decided that for reasons of tribal politics it must go on. If it is stopped the hot-heads will say that it is just another way of us destroying their tribal tradition."

"Bastards," said the man with feeling. "The bloody politicians are too scared to take part themselves, but are quite prepared to see the old men die."

"Yes, they are all you say. But I am as bad. If it goes on without the young politicians taking part, tribally they are finished."

"You're a cynical lot all right, you officials. I don't envy you your job. Better you than me," and before they could go on, the first of the guests began to arrive.

Next morning the man slept late and joined the D.C. in his office after a late breakfast.

"In your debt again," he said. "My thanks as always."

"Don't thank me. Thank Mary, as I expect you already have," was the reply. "We need a bit of company to keep us half sane. Sit down a minute if you have time. I have been thinking about the chila. I shall be there of course, and I would like you to be there too."

The man looked at him in surprise. "I thought that this was a very private tribal thing with no outsiders except yourself," he said.

"True," replied his friend, "but I feel that we need a couple of chaps who can shoot and what is more have the right weapons to shoot with, and who can keep cool. We might be able to save some damage that way and even some lives. I don't shoot as you know, and old Jack cannot cope with the area involved on his own." (Jack was the Game Ranger.) "The Chief and the others know you. I would count it as a favour if you would be there."

The man stood up, and stretching out his hand shook his friend's firmly.

"See you in October, John. Just give me a couple of days' warning," and he limped off to the car.

Chapter 27

Waiting

It was hot as only an October morning can be hot in the Ila country. The sun beat down mercilessly from the clear blue sky, and there was no evidence of the cloud build-up which would come later in the day. This gathering of clouds would increase day by day, bringing humidity and closeness until the heavy black banks of thunder clouds flashed and rolled and the long-awaited rain hissed down onto the dry earth below. But this would not be for several weeks yet. This morning it was hot where the man was sitting in his Landrover, now stripped down and completely open. He was at his favourite view point in the klipspringer hills, Robert beside him. It would be even hotter when they dropped down on to the forest far below. All they could see in front of them was a shimmering flatness in which few details could be made out in the heat haze apart from an ocasional very large baobab tree. Even the big hill where the Game Guard's camp was shivered and jumped in the heat and was very indistinct.

There were no klipslingers around today. There was no sign of any life at all. Tiny puffs of wind stirred the tree tops, whilst the trees themselves seemed to wilt in the heat. Nothing else moved, until the man jammed his hat hard onto his head and impatiently pushed up his dark glasses which kept slipping down his nose in a pool of sweat. He eased the vehicle down the hill and they were glad of the resulting movement of air against their faces. They arrived at the Game Guard's camp, but did not stay long there as he had already left to join Jack at the Chila. They greeted his wife and children, left presents and pushed on.

The man was horrified at the effects of the drought. From the hills he had looked for the smoke of bush fires and had been surprised to see none. Now he knew why. Everything readily inflammable had been burnt long ago in July and August and there was nothing left except dried cracked blackened soil in the mopane and dirty looking grey sand elsewhere, the general drabness being relieved only by the startling white ash of the remains of a mopane tree or a leadwood which had been reduced to powder by the intense heat of the bush fire that had consumed it.

There was no sign of any water in the river of course, and the man began to wonder when he would see pools with enough water to support the game. Certainly not at the wildebeeste pool. It was dry, cracked and desolate, and beside it lay the pathetic dehydrated body of a hartebeest, swollen tongue protruding. It was not long dead. There were no vultures. Perhaps the body was too far from water. The man walked a couple of hundred yards to the next pool to see what it was like. It had a darkening of the soil in its exposed bed, and here a few warthog were digging and rooting with tusk and muzzle to get at what moisture there was, and were reduced to sucking the turned-up soil. A few guinea fowl scratched amongst the turned-up soil too, seeking something to eat.

Now that he realised the extent of the dryness the man got out his map and plotted a route straight across country to the place on the Kavuvu plains where he knew the D.C. was camping, knowing that there was nothing to stop the vehicle, and they set off again. Eventually they passed near to the Mission and were glad to see that the permanent pools there still had water, living up to their name, though the man had never seen them so low. It seemed likely that these pools were fed by springs because further on the pools were dry again. They topped up the radiator and poured water from the pools over each other, clothes and all, the better to cool themselves, and drove on, travelling becoming a little more bearable as the heat went out of the sun. Soon they emerged onto the flood plain and they caught occasional glimpses of the D.C.'s camp in the middle distance through the long grass, not burnt here, which reached well over their heads as they drove along. They eventually arrived. The D.C. was not a man to forgo the niceties of civilisation easily, especially when they affected his comfort, and had brought along a paraffin 'fridge, and he was able to press an ice cold beer into the man's hand as he stepped from the vehicle. Jack was there too, and they sat and chatted as the light began to fade, gazing at the tree line which marked the Kavuvu five miles away across the grass. All was still and peaceful, but somewhere between themselves and the trees were the buffalo, some six hundred of them, hidden in the grass. The three were alone, the D.C. having rigidly excluded all people with no business to be there. Even his own staff was reduced to two servants, and these, and Robert and the two Game Guards, sat around their own little fire a little apart from the three Europeans eating and, drinking the one cold beer the D.C. had given them and talking quietly.

Beyond them, a quarter of a mile away, was the camp of the Ila warriors and their wives and attendants. There were a few more hardy souls there who had joined the twelve, none of them young. Their camp was not silent, for though the people had little to say and the warriors ate and drank without appetite the Chief's drummers were there, and the drums throbbed gently but persistently on the edge of the camp. Mukadi and the Chief sat together, the others grouped around them, talking softly amongst themselves and idly honing spear blades already sharp as razors. Mukadi began to speak, and they all listened, even the Chief who deferred to Mukadi in all matters pertaining to hunting.

"You must try and sleep," he was saying, "though I myself have never been able to do so before a chila. But we are old men anyway and need little sleep when the long eternal sleep is near to us."

He went on, "Let me explain again to you what will happen tomorrow, for the last time, and then we will forget about the chila until we are out there facing the buffalo. About four in the morning the people already gathered on the far bank of the Kavuvu with their canoes, will cross and will light the grass along the river bank for a mile or so, between the buffalo and the river. This we will see and we will also hear their drums. When this line of grass is well alight the people will begin to walk away from the river at each end of the fire, lighting the grass as they go. These two side lines are to contain the buffalo, and the people lighting the fires will gradually move closer to each other forming a long narrowing funnel or unburnt grass, the only exit being at the apex, which will be about a quarter of a mile across. The buffalo will be driven, not by the people but by the fire and smoke down the ever-narrowing funnel, and there at the exit we shall be waiting for them." He paused, and then went on, "but it is not as easy as that. When the fires are lit in the dark there will be no wind, but as the fires grow the wind will begin and with the wind will come the smoke, blinding and choking not only the buffalo but ourselves, so that the animals could come at us with little or no warning, appearing like ghosts out of the smoke. Then is the time for coolness. Do not be tempted to spear the buffalo from the front. Let them pass and stab with the short spear behind the shoulder as they do so. Do not throw unless you have to, and do not exult over the one you kill or mortally wound, but be ready for the next." He paused again and then said, "I beg of you to leave White Tail to me even if it means letting him past. You all know that I must kill him and why. Now Chief, what is the news of the cattle?" and he would allow no more talk of the coming ordeal.

No-one slept, and later in the night the medicine men came with their unguents, herbs and decoctions anxious to doctor the warriors with them, chanting and saying that their medicines would keep the warriors safe and free from injury and death, but Mukadi had no patience with them and asked them, if their medicine was so good why they did not doctor each other and, being safe, stand with the warriors next day. He had no takers, and the doctors left, humiliated and unforgiving, but Mukadi was past caring. Thereafter they chatted the night away talking of their cattle and other pleasant subjects.

White Tail

Neither did the Europeans sleep. The man had tried to relax on his camp bed, but the heat made rest impossible and he had rejoined the others sitting round the camp fire drinking endless cups of tea and watching the thin blue smoke rise straight upwards from the embers into the canopy of brilliant stars which sparkled clearly in spite of the moonlight. Even the constant throbbing of the drums lost its soporific effect as they waited.

The man, only half awake, felt a gentle tap on his shoulder.

"They are lighting the fires, Bwana," said Robert.

* * *

The buffalo were not uneasy. they had passed a normal night in the long grass, grazing, chewing the cud or just dozing. They were well hidden and only an occasional hump showed above a patch of grass a little shorter than the rest, looking like some whale broaching in a yellow sea. No predators had worried them and now instinct told them that it would soon be time to go to the river to drink. The only other animals to be seen dimly in the moonlight were some hippos, out on the bank grazing the grass there until it was like a lawn.

The matriarch of the herd, with the cows and youngsters which were her prime responsibility would drink first whilst White Tail and the bulls kept watch, and then later they would drink before they all moved off to the safety of the grass again, where they would spend the day patiently waiting, like eveything else in the bush, for the rains which would free them from the river and allow them to go back into the shady forests they loved. The matriarch began moving her charges towards the water as usual, but this was no ordinary day and she sensed that something was wrong. As they got near the bank she heard muffled sounds from the river and as she snorted her alarm the thing she feared most flared up in front of her, and broke out at many points along the bank and rapidly coalesced as the Ila ran along the edge of the grass dragging their flaming bundles of grass along the ground beside them. The herd milled round her seeking a lead, and her first instinct was to turn and flee, but something told her that this would be wrong, and White Tail and the bulls, grouped further away, saw her lead her charges in an irresistible wild stampede through the wall of flame to the river and safety. They crossed to the plains on the other side but did not stop, continuing their gallop until they were well away from the river. Two or three calves were drowned and three old Ila who had been attending the canoes were overwhelmed and killed in the stampede.

Seeing the bulk of the herd escape through the flames White Tail decided to lead his bulls after them, but by the time he reached the wall of fire nothing could pass through, and the shouting and drumming beyond the fire made him turn away. Far away to his left and right the fire stretched and he saw that it was also moving inland from his flanks as if to surround the bulls eventually, and at a trot he led them away from the river towards the only place where there was apparently no fire.

Chapter 28

The Chila

When Robert had alerted the man, he and his companions made their way to the spots they had chosen, with some care, the evening before, to occupy during the chila. Where the buffalo would pass through their gap to freedom the plain was dotted with large termite mounds, as big as native huts, jutting up above the grass. There was a good view from their tops, and they were obviously places of relative safety. Robert, the man and the D.C. went to one which was a third of the way across the gap, and Jack and his two men to one similarly situated on the other side, so that the two men with rifles could cover the area well.

The Ila used the mounds too, taking up their positions not on them but in front, so that when the buffalo came they had to pass to the side to get round the mound, thereby exposing their vulnerable flanks. They strung themselves across the gap and the man could see the Chief a hundred yards or so from him, and beyond him Mukadi. In the early morning light their tall head dresses, seldom worn now, waved high above the grass and the man could clearly see the red and blue feathers in their headbands. He knew that all the Ila would strive for another or perhaps their first red feather today.

He could hear the drumming and the shouting beyond the distant flames, and he had the heavy rifle loaded and ready. The D.C. was doing his nonchalant British Official act, and was seated as comfortably as he could be reading an old copy of Blackwood's. Robert held the man's shotgun. There was no sign of buffalo, but as the flames came nearer and the thick smoke swirled around, the large tail-less Shakalongo and four other lions trotted through the gap, ignoring the Ila and the Ila ignored them. The man's finger itched on the trigger, but a shot now would turn or distract the buffalo. Then at last, through the smoke and dust they saw the first of the buffalo half a mile away, coming to them at a fast trot. They were hard to see in the long grass and the smoke, but as they approached the man shouted above the din,

White Tail

"A wash out; there are only about fifty. The rest must have broken back early on."

"Good," replied the D.C., "I'm glad. I don't see why the poor beasts should be shot for an Ila holiday," but further philosophising was cut short by the crack of a rifle from Jack's side, and they saw a buffalo stagger and fall. Then everything seemed to happen at once. The leading animals began to gallop, and a huge bull made for the Chief, who, not withstanding Mukadi's advice, flung his spear harmlessly at the animal head on and was tossed. He hit the ground, and as the buffalo turned to gore him the man fired, dropping it dead beside the unconscious Chief.

Now the buffalo panicked, and another bull made straight for Mukadi. He stood coolly, and through the smoke the man admired the way he let it past and killed it with one thrust of the spear. This he extracted from the dying animal and turned to the man shaking his spear in exultation. It was then that the second bigger buffalo, its white tail streaming behind, killed him, and before the man could fire the smoke shut out the sight, and the buffalo and the rest of the herd were through the line and free.

* * *

They found Mukadi at the foot of the termite mound looking frail and small in death. His spear was still in his hand, and if his face showed anything at all it was surprise. The man wondered if he had seen the white tail before he died. No-one would ever know. The Chief, conscious but broken in spirit as well as in body, was carried over to his old friend, and wept when he saw him.

Presently he spoke to the man. "You know his senior wife. She is your friend as you were his. Chipimo is already dead, and she will not mind what I do now, and our dead friend would have approved," and he removed the headband and the red and blue feathers from the body and handed them to the man.

"Remember him by these, his most cherished possessions," he went on. "You are one of the few who knew the story of White Tail and Mukadi's curse. The old doctor was right. When Mukadi saw White Tail his bad luck ended, but not in the way we all expected. Remember all this well, for the story will become an Ila legend. The story of White Tail is not yet ended, and it is in my mind that you will see the end of it." And with great dignity he bade the three Europeans farewell, and had his bearers carry him off to his camp and his agony.

* * *

That evening, when all the fires on the plain had been beaten out and the wailing and mourning had begun in the Ila camp, the three white men sat around their fire, their servants nearby.

The Chila

"So," said the D.C., "Three killed at the river and Mukadi killed here. The Chief and two others badly maimed, and only three buffalo killed. That's four to three to the buffalo I reckon, and considering you two killed one each it is really four to one. I think now that I can persuade even the politicians and officials that the chila must end. It is only too bad that four men had to die to make the point."

The D.C. got his way, and the man was always thankful that he had seen the last one, a thing that few non Ila had ever seen.

PART 5   OLD AGE

Chapter 29
White Tail leaves the herd

The flickering of the newly lit fires seemed only to make the darkness darker as the Ila lit them at the beginning of the Chila, but having assessed the situation correctly the herd matriarch led her charges fearlessly into the void beyond the flames. The river bank was some fifteen feet high at this point and the buffalo poured over it like lemming over a cliff, quickly breaking it down into a slope. The three old men guarding the canoes had just lit charcoal fires against the cold and never knew what hit them, and whether they were drowned or battered to death no-one would ever know. They were alive one minute and dead the next. The shallow river was no obstacle to the now panic-stricken buffalo, nor was the opposite bank, up which they streamed on to the plain beyond, never stopping until they reached the tree line two miles away.

When the herd had drawn breath and rested the matriarch set about the difficult task of bullying them into returning the way they had come. She knew that with the coming rains the river would rise quickly and they would be cut off from the bulls, which she realised had not followed them, until the river fell again. She could see across the plain the smoke and dust on the other side of the river and earlier she had heard faintly the shots. The rest of the herd were not at all keen to return, but by evening she had got them back to within a short distance of the river bank, by which time the noise and fire and smoke had died down. Next morning she led them over on to the black, dusty, smokey desolation of ash that only the day before had been a yellow sea of grass. She had no way of knowing which way the bulls had gone, but by luck and by staying to the burnt area she picked up their spoor by midday, and followed it to the forest. The acrid smoke and dust made scenting almost impossible, but having found the spoor she never lost it again, and came up with the bulls four days later, near the buffalo pool.

White Tail was glad to see the herd matriarch leading the buffaloes to the re-uniting of the herd for more reasons than one. His bulls were edgy and nervous, milling round in a startled fashion at the least thing that upset them, and being apparently ready to stampede at any time. They had had a far harder time of the Chila than the cows, and the appearance of these, with the yearlings and calves, did something to begin a calming process which would last many weeks. But at last White Tail and the matriarch restored the herd discipline, and early and good rains that year cooled tempers as well as bodies. There was no migratory trip to the west that year. White Tail kept the herd deep in the forest near the buffalo pool, avoiding other herds, and leading them out on to the flats to graze as seldom as possible, and they remained undiscovered by hunter, poacher or traveller. So they recovered, and the next rains made the trip to the west and back, and prospered. Their only worry was the constant one of the lions, but this was part of their life.

One afternoon on the edge of the plains the herd was caught by a pride of twelve, two adult females, two adult lions and eight young males. These slaughtered eight adult buffalo, far more than they needed to eat, and all that day and through the following day the scavengers gorged themselves, so that the vultures could not fly and even the hyaenas had had enough.

Another time they were attacked by Shakalongo, once so formidable and now a toothless bag of bones, abandoned by his fellows, and starving. He attacked in a foolish frenzy, half crazed by hunger, and was easily killed by one of the younger bulls which would have had no chance against him in his prime. The bull did not even need any assistance from White Tail or the others, though they all took turns at goring and tossing the body.

But generally the herd led a quiet and peaceful existence, and prospered, so that now, four years after the Chila, White Tail was overlord of nearly a thousand animals. This was far too many, and he was glad when one of the other bulls took off a couple of hundred of them to start a new herd, and another bull took away another hundred. Had they not done so there would have been a fight for the leadership of a herd already too large for one master, which would have benefitted none, and so the defectors went peacefully, unchallenged by White Tail. He, however realised that the time was near when he would be challenged. There had been a few half-hearted attempts already, but

White Tail leaves the herd

since White Tail was still the biggest in the herd in spite of his age, none had been pressed home.

He was undeniably getting old and was greatly changed. The jet black glossy coat no longer shone in the sun, but was a hairless dirty grey, and the once startling white tail was now sparsely haired, though still white. Only the yellow or red bills of the ever-present oxpeckers gave a little colour to him. Nor did he hold up proudly and arrogantly the huge head with the formidable heavily bossed horns which were now worn and splintered. It was too heavy even for that massive neck, and his head mostly hung down in a dejected fashion, and though his neck and shoulders were still a mass of muscle his rump was gaunt and the bones stuck out pathetically. Formidable though he still was he was now content to leave more and more of his duties to the matriarch and his lieutenants, for even procreation bored and tired him now.

The half-expected challenge came one morning near the buffalo pool. With failing eyesight and hearing, but still with a keen sense of smell, White Tail had been approaching a cow in season, and neither saw nor heard the assailant who butted him hard in the side. He spun round very quickly for so big an animal and for a few seconds it looked as though there would be a fight to the death. He clashed head on with his challenger, driving him back on his haunches, and there was a flicker of fear in the young bull's eyes, but though the strength was still there White Tail's spirit was gone, and he turned away before his challenger could recover, and trotted off, past the other bulls who had gathered for the fight, and thus left the herd in which he had lived all his life, and which he had led so long and so well. He made off, knowing exactly where he was going, and very soon joined three other old bulls who lived together a mile or so away from the main herd. Four lions following the bulls, beginning to feel that they might now be decrepit enough to attack, were not pleased to see the relatively strong newcomer join them, and decided that the odds were no longer in their favour and that they would have a better chance of eating safely if they stalked the main herd. The three bulls welcomed White Tail and they felt somehow safer, knowing that four of them, back to back, could form a tight defensive circle against the bosses and horns of which only the most intrepid attacker would persist. They would live securely together until old age or disease took them. White tail felt strangely content, and was happy as he followed the others to a small dense thicket, around which the ground was plastered with dung, indicating a favourite and safe resting place for the old bulls during the day. Only a rhino might want to use such a small dense thicket, but the rhino were a little further north in their own thicket stronghold. Many said that they no longer lived in the Kavuvu area. Others, including the man, knew better, but they kept the knowledge to themselves so that the animals could increase and be safe from the biologists who would want to count, measure, and otherwise disturb and harass them, and from the poachers who wanted them for their horns with their reputedly aphrodisiac properties. So this was where the four old bulls lived, spending their days either in the cool safety of the thicket or in the nearby grasslands, sleeping a lot, dozing on their feet, disturbed by neither man nor beast, happy in their senescence.

Chapter 30

The Last Big Walk

Apart from an occasional sparkle of sunlight on the river far below nothing moved under the pitiless heat of the sun, not even the man who was sitting high on the hill overlooking the gap. It was very hot and the glare was almost as bad as the heat, hurting the eyes unless they were protected. There was no wind and the sweat poured from the man. Looking over the flats towards the Island the heat haze made the trees shimmer as though they were a mirage and not real, so that they appeared to float above the ground. The man was indulging himself, gazing, as he had done so often before from this favourite spot, at nothing in particular, but missing nothing.

Today no animal moved and no bird either, except for two bateleur eagles circling above the river but below the man. His rifle and cromach were at hand as usual, and he was deceiving himself into believing that he was watching vigilantly, but in fact he was half asleep, drowsy because of the heat and tired from the morning's walk from the Island where he had been fishing for a few days, and the climb up the hill.

Robert, who had come up from their camp a little further down the hill, touched him gently on the shoulder.

"Sleep properly, Bwana," he said. "I will keep watch. There is plenty of time to sit here in the evening when it is cool."

"Perhaps you are right," the man replied, and, finding a reasonably comfortable piece of ground, he stretched out, thinking to himself, "My God, I must be getting old. I never heard him."

He slept heavily and when he awoke there was a mug of tea beside him and the evening was much cooler. It was now after five, and he could see game far below, moving towards the water.

But the man was not happy at this spot he loved so much and of

The Last Big Walk

which he thought he could never tire. He knew that this would probably be his last time up there. It had not been a good day. The walk and the climb had played havoc with his knee, and he realised that the pleasure of long walks was now outweighed by the subsequent pain and stiffness. True he could use the Land Rover to visit the bush, but it was not the same, and even that vehicle could not get to places like the top of the hill where he now sat. He was not, however, one to brood over the impossible, and having decided that walking was now a thing of the past, he put it from his mind, and instead devoted his attention to the fiery orb of the sun setting over the flat forest, marvelling not for the first time at the flash of green amongst the reds and oranges just before it disappeared.

He had originally intended to walk to the buffalo pool and camp at the nearby haunted camp, but now decided to walk only as far as the Game Guards' camp where he had left the Land Rover, perhaps visiting the abandoned ruined Mission on the way. This was a good twelve miles, but a very early start would avoid the worst of the heat. He ate what Robert had prepared for him and fell asleep, whilst Robert sat for a while gazing into the fire.

It was barely light next morning when they slipped down the hill. It was pleasantly cool and the man's depression of the previous night had evapourated. He had a feeling that it was going to be a good day, this last day of walking in the bush, and said as much to Robert.

Reaching the foot of the hill they struck off westwards, making for the old road where they had seen the honey badger many years ago, and in spite of his knee the man stepped out, driving himself along with his cromach. Nevertheless they went with due care, knowing that they were not the only ones abroad so early. But apart from a small herd of elephant bulls which made them wait as they crossed in front of them nothing disturbed them, and they soon reached the road, and turned south towards the Game Guards' camp.

It was truly a wonderful morning. They were walking through mopane woodland liberally dotted with baobab trees, grotesque and huge, bare of leaves but carrying silvery-white buds on long swinging stalks, some of which had already burst into dazzling white flowers. As it got hotter the butterfly-like leaves of the mopane began to close, and the pods still remaining on the trees were more easily seen, but there were not many. There was very little grass. What had escaped the bush fires had been grazed flat by the abundant game, and this lack of grass combined with the fact that neither of the main trees had low spreading branches enabled the men to see far between them and thus enjoy the sight of what seemed to be almost limitless game. The man was euphoric as he walked along.

White Tail

Robert and the man saw the wild dog at the same time, each grasping the other's elbow to warn the other. There were eight of them trotting across their front a hundred yards ahead and the man readied the rifle, for a pack of African hunting dogs is a formidable opponent. He raised his binoculars and, handing them to Robert, said, "It's all right. Look well. They have already killed and eaten but not yet drunk. They are covered with blood. Nothing for us to worry about. It *is* a good day, Robert. We are lucky to see them." And his luck held. The pack stopped and turned their heads as one towards the two men, gazing at them curiously, quite without fear and without any sign of aggression, before walking on, slowly now. Except for one. She walked off to the side a few yards. "That one is not all right, Bwana," said Robert, pointing with his chin. "Look. She is vomiting."

"No. It is not that. Look through the glasses again. We are going to see something interesting," replied the man, and as he spoke four pups came tumbling out of a clump of grass making a bee line for the fresh meat that their mother had carried from the kill and had regurgitated for them. They attacked the meat in the ferocious manner of their kind whilst the mother lay panting a few feet away waiting for the attack on her dugs which would come as soon as the meat was eaten. The rest, too, lay down, and made no move except with their eyes and heads as the men made their way past them, still curious, still unaggressive.

After the encounter with the wild dog the country began to change from open woodland to thicket which was claustrophobic in its thickness and which stretched, as the man knew, almost to their destination, the Game Guards' camp. It was terrible country to walk through and had it not been for the road it would hav been impossible. At least it gave them shade. It was the haunt of elephant and rhino, both of which appreciated it for the cover and therefore protection it gave them, they being the only animals able to move through it easily. Even the buffalo shunned it. The man saw plenty of signs of both, but never the animals, though once they heard the hurried crashing of some large animal away from them as they walked along. The only thing they saw, and it was only a glimpse, was a leopard which slipped across the road in front of them, a dead guinea fowl in its mouth.

A couple of miles further along the man began to pay closer attention to the bush on his left, and soon gave a grunt of satisfaction.

"Here we are, Robert," he said. "This is what I am looking for," pointing to a narrow but well used game trail going off to their left. They turned down it and for a time the going was difficult indeed, but eventually the thicket began to thin out and they were able to walk upright again. The man stopped in a small clearing.

The Last Big Walk

"Recognise this place, Robert?," he asked, and receiving only a blank look went on, "This is where we caught Mukadi and the boy and released the waterbuck. We have been coming down the track the waterbuck use to get to the river."

"Yes, now I see," replied Robert. "We are not far from the old Mission, then?"

"True. Let's get there and eat. I'm hungry."

They sat and ate their frugal lunch sitting on the exposed foundation stones of what had once been the small church. Around them were the remains, little more than a few small pathetic heaps of stone, of what had been the houses, and beyond them were the headstones of the graves. The whole was in a clearing shaded by huge fig trees, through which was the magnificent view of the river and swamp a hundred yards away, which had seduced the missionaries with its beauty and killed them with its mosquitoes, some immediately and some months later when they had been forced to abandon the site.

They reminisced about Mukadi and the boy, remembering unimportant things like finding the head of the barbel the otters had stolen from the old Ila's line, until Robert said, "Remember the white-tailed one that killed them, Bwana? I wonder what happened to him."

"Must be dead now or very old," replied the man. "He was a lucky one though, from the time you pulled him from the mud when he was a calf, to the time he escaped in the smoke from the Chila."

Lunch over they quickly covered the remaining distance to the camp walking through the meadows beside the little river which was now more of a line of isolated pools than a stream. There they were met by the Game Guard, their old friend, now moved from the isolated post in the south to this busier and more important one.

"I see you, Bwana. I see you Robert," he said, obviously delighted. "I have your Land Rover safe here. But come and let us drink tea," and he led them to the shade of a large fig tree and called his wife to get the tea ready.

The man asked after his family, and the children were now grown up and away at school, but came home in the holidays, walking from the Government station where the school was if they could not get a lift, totally unafraid in the bush.

The man then told of their walk and of what they had seen in the way of game, which was important to the guard. He was interested that there were wild dog in the district, for they were seldom seen and even more rarely reported.

"So what are your plans now?" the game guard asked.

"No more walking I am afraid," and the game guard nodded. He knew all about the knee. "I'll drive down to the haunted camp and spend a couple of days there seeing what there is to see and having a look at the buffalo pool."

"Rather you then me," was the reply, and Robert nodded miserably in agreement. "Is it true that the Spirits do not worry the white man, or that white men do not have ancestral Spirits?"

The man laughed. "When I came here I thought that they didn't, but now I'm not so sure. Remember how we all mocked the old doctor who foretold the buffalo that had the white tail? No-one believed him, but he was right and the buffalo did for Mukadi all right and fulfilled the old man's prophecy. So I don't know. But I no longer scoff. Did you ever hear any more about White Tail?"

The game guard replied indirectly. "When you get to the haunted camp you will go to the buffalo pool. Look well in that area. A poacher I caught last week reported seeing him with two other old bulls, apart from the herd now. Knowing his story and believing the buffalo to be magic as all the locals do after the killing of Mukadi he hurried out of the area so carelessly that he ran straight into one of my scouts and was caught. He is quite sure of his facts, so you may see White Tail."

They then chatted of other things, but the man's mind was not on anything they said. He wanted to see White Tail again.

It had been a good day though, as he thought.

Chapter 31

The Death of White Tail

The man had only intended to spend a couple of days at the haunted camp and had driven there very confident that he would pick up White Tail's tracks and see the old buffalo, probably for the last time. It did not work out that way at all.

It got hotter and hotter as the days passed, and in spite of using the Land Rover over the bone dry plains and through what parts of the forests they could, they saw no trace of the three bulls, though twice they saw large herds of buffalo. Heavy-looking black rain clouds built up each afternoon, only to disappear during the following night, but on the evening of the third day of fruitless searching the heavens opened. Watching the rain pour down from the dry comfort of their hut as the light went the man and Robert realised that the rain was a mixed blessing. It had cooled things down a lot, making life much more bearable, but if it persisted the game, buffalo included, would scatter. Further, they would be very restricted in the use of their vehicle, and would perhaps have to get out whilst the going was literally good.

There was now some urgency about their search, and when they set off on foot before sun-up next morning they went in a new direction, westwards away from the buffalo pool along an old half-forgotten overgrown footpath which led eventually to a small camp twenty miles away which was not usually occupied, but used only by Game Guards when on tour. The previous night's rain had made for a very misty morning, and before the sun appeared it was very thick. Tall palms seemed to float mysteriously in the haze and at their feet scattered over the plain like wraiths were the roan antelope and their attendant impala. Later they would go their separate ways, but at this early hour they liked each other's company. Wherever there was a watercourse reedbuck lay, reluctant to rise and leave their forms until they felt the sun on their backs.

Though the rain was a threat to their search, it did give the man some immediate help by making the dusty sand firm, so that it fixed well, for a while at least, the tracks of all the creatures which had passed along or across the track during the night. Two honey badgers had been there and so had a porcupine. Here and there were the delicate paw marks of serval cats, and once they saw the pug marks of a leopard which had followed the track for a long distance. They saw too the unmistakable spoor of an antbear, a creature the man had never seen in the flesh; but interesting as this story was so clearly written on the ground they did not see what they were looking for until the sun was well up, and then they saw the cloven spoor of two buffalo crossing in front of them. No wind had as yet blunted the sharp edges of the tracks and no rain had blurred them. Sharply and deeply etched into the ground they were not more than half an hour old.

"Two buffalo," said the man. "Probably old bulls judging by the size of the spoor. Not more than half an hour ago I would say. It could be White Tail. Let's go. You spoor first and I'll follow."

"But the poacher told the Game Guard that there were three of them," said Robert.

"That was over a week ago. Lions could have got one. Keep your eyes open for lion spoor too," said the man, talking in the staccato way he had when he was excited.

They set off into the bush and the signs were clear even there and easy to follow. They got along quickly, and had not gone more than half a mile when they found a pat of dung. The man felt it with the back of his hand.

"Warm," he said quietly. "Slowly now," and they went on even more carefully, a gentle breeze occasionally blowing into their faces as the sun rose, the rifle ready.

After a silent ten minutes the man stopped.

"They are near, Robert. I can smell them," he said as he caught a whiff of the familiar pungent cattle smell, and as he spoke he saw them.

"There," he whispered to Robert, pointing with his chin in the African way, and sure enough there they were, two big bulls, standing placidly enough beneath a clump of mopane trees. Flies were already bothering them, and as they swished their tails it was easy to see that they had found what they sought.

The buffalo showed no sign that they knew that the men were there. Hardly daring to move the man watched them for a good half hour until cramp and stiffness got the better of him. He then stood up and slapped the butt of the rifle. They saw and heard immediately, looking keenly at the two men, and then with great dignity and without haste trotted ponderously off amongst the trees.

"We will have a last look at them tomorrow," said the man. "They will not go far, and unless there is a very heavy rain, which I doubt, we shall pick them up again without any trouble," and they walked back to the camp, where, apart from working on the Land Rover and fishing in the pool in front of the huts, they passed a lazy day and were in bed as soon as darkness fell.

It was not a restful night. The man fell quickly and deeply asleep, but was wakened by the noise of lions, not far away, growling, roaring and grunting, the uproar being compounded by the shrieks, giggles and whooping of numerous hyaenas. The lions apparently were not successful in their hunting, for the racket went on and on. Obviously no kill had been made. The man switched on his torch and found that he had only been asleep for a couple of hours, but eventually in spite of the noise he slept, and the next time he woke it was to see Robert heating water over the petrol stove by the light of a candle. He pulled on his clothes and, as was his invariable habit, shaved. He never went out however wild the bush and however early it might be without doing so, a quirk he attributed to a subconscious respect for some long-forgotten colonel or adjutant.

"Morning Robert. Did you sleep well?"

"Not very, Bwana, what with the lions and the spooks." He was convinced that the noises of the night were not made by hyaenas but by ghosts. "I hope that the lions have not driven the buffalo away."

"I hope not. In any case we must be careful this morning," replied the man, and he loaded the big rifle and set off with it in the crook of his right arm, grasping the cromach with his left, but ready to drop it at the first hint of trouble. It was barely light. There were six elephants in the

The Death of White Tail

pool in front of the huts, but they were intent on their own affairs, and took no notice of the men as they moved away from them. By the time they could see clearly they were where they had left the buffalo the previous day.

It was eight lionesses who had been making all the noise in the early part of the night, and nothing had gone right for them. Dozing roan antelope had sensed them and galloped off, snorting with alarm, not stopping until they had put more than a mile between themselves and the lionesses. Impala had heard them and had flitted off through the trees like silent ghosts. An old warthog had eluded them and had backed down into an abandoned burrow, his formidable tusks facing the exit. An antbear, the lions' favourite prey, had also escaped to another burrow and was still there, warm, dry, and safe. The lionesses had seen no buffalo, and were not sorry. They were a pride of eight, all females and no cubs with them. There were two old ones, wise and seasoned hunters and had they been on their own they would not have been hungry, but they were the mentors for the other six which were much younger and, about two years old, were learning their job of killing to survive.

It was just getting light when one of the old ones caught the faintest whiff of buffalo. She alerted the others and, her senses sharpened by hunger, led them on slowly and carefully until in a small open area amongst the mopane she saw White Tail and his companion. Her tail lashed, but she was not happy. The odds on an easy kill were poor. Two old buffalo bulls were not suitable prey for young lionesses learning their business. However it was a choice between killing now or going hungry until the next night, and the old lioness's foodless belly overruled her natural caution. There was no wind, and taking advantage of this she began, like some feline general, to dispose her forces, and soon the buffalo, still unsuspecting, were surrounded by the unseen cats. Satisfied, the old one gave a grunting cough and showed herself, alerting the buffalo which moved away from her, only to discover that there were lionesses all round them. They stood back to back, insufficient to form a defensive circle, and prepared to fight it out.

The man, alert for lions, heard the old female cough and grunt not far ahead and made his way cautiously forward, Robert just behind him. He was soon able to pick out the lionesses and beyond them the buffalo on which they were intent. He watched the manoeuvres of the old lioness with interest, and thought that the odds were about even. She had no intention of attacking herself. The two old ones were there as teachers, and, having made her dispositions, she hung back and encouraged the youngsters to attack. Had they all rushed in together things might have gone better for them, but two of the more bold went in together, galloping with stiff tails, but foolishly straight for White Tail. The leader attempted to force herself past the horns and was tossed for her pains, roaring with pain and anger as her ribs broke. Her companion took advantage of White Tail's preoccupation to jump on his shoulders, seeking desperately with teeth and claws for the neck. Her inexperience led to her downfall, and the other buffalo hooked her off White Tail's back, his old horns, broken and splintered, inflicting a trerrible wound as they ripped open her abdomen. This was the old lioness's chance and she did not hesitate, but led the others in and attacked the buffalo as it gored their companion, and, overwhelming him by sheer weight of numbers, messily and slowly killed him, whilst White Tail made off, bleeding profusely from the rips on his shoulders. The lions that were left began to feed on their buffalo and also on their dead companion. The one with the broken ribs crawled painfully away and was killed and eaten by hyaenas the following night.

The man had watched fascinated. He had been tempted to interfere, but being used to the cruelties of Nature he resisted and did nothing. He watched the lionesses feed, their dead and wounded companions already forgotten, and saw White Tail move slowly away. Leaving the carnage behind them, he and Robert quietly followed.

But the day's excitement was not yet over, they had not been the only spectators. Four lions, full grown and magnificent, had seen the fight, and seeing the buffalo killed, their leader had just decided to take them and drive the females off the kill when he saw that the surviving buffalo, bleeding freely from his shoulders, was staggering straight towards the lions. It was an easy kill not to be missed. The man saw the lions rush out on White Tail and thought "This is too much," and raised his rifle. The leader was very quickly on the buffalo's shoulders, and with one claw firmly on the muzzle was trying hard to break his adversary's neck by twisting it viciously, his hind claws ripping and tearing the flanks whilst the other lions snapped and tore at his hind legs trying to hamstring him. The heavy bullet from the left barrel of the rifle smashed the leader's head to pulp, and White Tail, freed from the weight of his attackers, turned slowly to get at the lions at his rear. They, startled and puzzled by the shot, had backed off. But White Tail was done for, and he knew nothing of the bullet from the other barrel which smashed the bones of his neck, so that he dropped as though pole-axed, the white tail stiff and quivering. The man reloaded, but the lions had had enough and made for the easier feeding with the females.

"I should not have interfered, Robert," said the man, "but we have known the old white-tailed one for a long time and he had had enough."

Robert said nothing, and the man squatted, leaning on the rifle, looking at the dead buffalo and thinking of all the years he had known

The Death of White Tail

him, and of the men who had been his friends killed by him, and of the many lions he must have killed, and of the bawling white-tailed calf Robert had pulled from the mud. And now it was ended.

Robert grasped him by the elbow and lifted him gently.

"Come, Bwana," he said, "Let's go. It is finished now," and the two friends moved off towards their camp, sad but once again alert and watchful.

References

The Ila-speaking people of N. Rhodesia	Smith and Dale
PUKU (the journal of the Wild Life Department of Zambia)	Vols 1 to 7
The East African Wildlife Journal	Vols 1 and 4
The Larger Mammals of Africa	Dorst and Dandelot
Mammals of N. Rhodesia	Ansell
Mammals of Zambia	Ansell
Animals of Rhodesia	Astley Maberly
Birds of Zambia	Dowsett, et. al.
Birds of South Africa	Roberts
Trees of Southern Africa	Keith, Coates & Palgrave
50 Common Trees of N. Rhodesia	Fanshawe
Know Your Trees	Storrs, for Forestry Department of Zambia
Some Common Trees and Shrubs of the Luangwa Valley	Carr
Snakes of Southern Africa	Fitzsimmons
The Fishes of N. Rhodesia	Jackson
Livingstone's Private Journals	ed Schapera
Black's Veterinary Dictionary	
Among the Elephants	Douglas-Hamilton
The Zoology of Tropical Africa	Cloudsley Thompson